STOKER

UNTAMED SONS MC SHORT STORY

JESSICA AMES

Emma,
Lovely to see you again!
enjoy the Ride
x

Copyright © 2022 by Jessica Ames

www.jessicaamesauthor.com

Stoker is a work of fiction. Names, places, characters and incidents are a product of the author's imagination and are fictitious. Any resemblance to actual persons, living or dead, events or establishments is solely coincidental.

Editing by Knox Publishing

Beta readers: Lynne Garlick, Clara Martinez Turco, Pat Labrie, Allisyn Pentleton

Please note this book contains material aimed at an adult audience, including sex, violence and bad language.

This book is licensed for your personal enjoyment. It may not be re-sold or given away to other people. If you would like to share this book with another person, please purchase an additional copy for each recipient. If you are reading this book and did not purchase it, or if it was not purchased for your use only, then you should return it to the seller and please purchase your own copy.

All rights reserved. Except as permitted under Copyright Act 1911 and the Copyright Act 1988, no part of this publication may be reproduced, distributed or transmitted in any form or by any means, or stored in a database or retrieval system, without the prior express, written consent of the author.

This book is covered under the United Kingdom's Copyright Laws. For more information visit: www.gov.uk/copyright/overview

AUTHOR'S NOTE

This book contains themes of murder, mayhem and other topics that may be upsetting. Reader discretion is advised.
https://www.jessicaamesauthor.com/jessicaamestwcw

This book is set in the United Kingdom. Some spellings may differ.

1

STOKER

THE FIRST BREATH of free air I take almost chokes me. Nothing has ever tasted sweeter. I tip my head back and let the sun shine on my face, soaking it in.

Fuck, that feels so good.

I let my eyes drift back towards the place I called home for the last nine years. I never thought this day would come, but as I stare up at the high walls looming behind me, I realise I'm finally a free man.

Freedom...

I had no idea how much I valued it until it was snatched from me. My life was taken from me in an instant, my liberty stripped away, and I became a number, an inmate, not a person. I was forced into a routine of someone else's making. I was forced to make friends with the right people to keep my back protected. I was forced to do terrible things to keep myself alive.

I should be celebrating my release, but what I feel is a little uncertain and a whole lot of fucking anxious. Everything feels open, exposed. It's been so long since I was last anywhere with this much open space. It threatens to overwhelm me.

I shift in my clothes, scratching at my chest. It's like a thousand fire ants are crawling over my skin. The denim of my jeans feels strange, coarse in a way I don't ever remember. Before I was locked up, I wore jeans every day, but I already miss the loose-fitting jogging pants that became a part of my everyday life during my stay at Her Majesty's pleasure.

I weave through the first row of cars, noticing there are a few models I don't recognise. Before I got locked up, I worked in the club's garage with Gasket and a few other brothers. I knew everything about cars then, but these ones seem foreign, strange to me.

Ignoring the pang in my chest, I peer around, looking for a familiar face, but I don't see anyone, so I lean against a low wall that surrounds the parking area. I let the noise of the traffic from the road just beyond the prison wash over me. It's quieter than the constant yelling from the inmates and the sound of doors slamming, keys scraping in the locks. It unsettles me in a way I didn't expect, and I have to take a steadying gulp of air to calm my racing heart.

"Stoker."

The sound of my name—the name given to me by the only family I've ever known—has my head snapping around.

It's then I see him.

Lennox Mathews, or Nox as he goes by in the club.

He looks the same as always—shaved head and eyes that look like they've seen into the pits of hell. Fuck, we all have that glint in our eyes. You don't become a member of an MC because you had a good upbringing. Each one of us came to the Untamed Sons to find something. I hadn't expected to find prison, but it is an occupational hazard. I was charged with assault. The judge threw the fucking book at me because of my club affiliations. Ten years inside—out in nine. It hadn't been easy, leaving my life behind, leaving my brothers and friends behind, but I'd done what I needed to for the club. Even when the pigs had offered to reduce my sentence if I gave them inside information, I hadn't.

I could hack time inside.

I couldn't hack being a rat.

My eyes are drawn to that leather kutte that covers Nox's torso. I can't see the back of it the way he's leaning against the cage he's standing next to, but I know what's on it. The skull wearing a crown with angel wings coming out of it. It's the same insignia that once sat on the back of my own kutte. I miss that piece of leather. For as long as I can remember, it's been like a second skin, fitting me like a glove.

I glance at the VP patch on the front of his kutte, and pain cracks my chest that I wasn't there to see him get it. I've known Nox a long time and I would have liked to see him making a name for himself.

Nox moved up to vice president a few years back, after Ravage's brother, Sin, raped his old lady, Sasha. I can't remember who told me that happened. It might have been Gasket or maybe Titch on one of their visits, but I knew Sash back in the day. She's a good woman, solid. Perfect for prez. She didn't deserve that shit. No one deserves to have their choice taken away like that. I can't even imagine what Ravage felt when he found out about it. I didn't know Sin had it in him to do something so fucking evil, and I'm guessing Rav never did either, but I know the Sons took care of it in a way that means Sin is pushing up fucking daisies somewhere.

I wonder what else has changed. I know the club won't be the same. The members will have changed, old ladies will have appeared, some vanishing off the scene for good, unable to hack the life. New faces will be among my brothers as the club has added to its ranks.

Not knowing what I'm walking into makes me nervous as fuck, especially since my life has been the same every day since I got locked up. I'm already feeling weird about not having my usual routine.

Despite my anxiety, my lips pull into a smirk, and as I get closer, Nox's smile gets wider.

"Motherfucker," he caws as he throws his arms around me and pulls me in for a back-slapping hug.

It's the first real contact I've had since I was jailed. I've had visitors, but the prison guards didn't like touching in case drugs were passed. It feels alien. Bizarre. For a moment, I don't return the hug, but then I let myself relax into it. It feels so good to have human contact again.

Nox pulls back from me, his grin still in place, and peers into my face, his eyes sparkling.

"Fuck, brother, you look good."

"Better than you," I joke.

He laughs. "Cunt." He slaps my back. "It's been too fucking long."

It has. Longer than I thought it would be. The club has good solicitors on the books, but even they couldn't work miracles. No one could undo the shit I got myself into.

"You ready to go home?" he asks.

Home.

Fuck.

I forgot what that word means. Home was a six-foot cell I shared with another inmate. It was the rec space that was never empty apart from after lights out and eating meals with fifty other men every day. Home was dodging shanks in the shower.

The thought of having my own space again seems unreal.

"Fuck, yeah," I say, ignoring the way my words catch in my throat.

He starts walking, and after a moment, I follow him. I feel

like a lost fucking puppy. Everything is the same but so different.

I'm different.

I'm not the same man who went inside. I'm harder. All my smooth edges chipped away. I thought I was a monster before I was incarcerated, but jail made me a new kind of beast, a different type of demon. My thoughts are shrouded in darkness, filled with pain and torment. I'm fucked in the head, broken, damaged, and I don't know if I'll ever be the same man I was before I went inside.

"Had the old ladies go in this morning and clean up your flat." Nox digs into his jeans pocket and tosses me a set of keys.

Coming back into the conversation, I instinctively flick out a hand and I catch them.

I stare at them for a moment before I raise my eyes back to his.

"They didn't have to do that," I mutter.

Nox looks at me like I'm fucking crazy. "They wanted to. You're fucking family, Stoker. We take care of our own."

That touches me more than I want to admit. Most of the brothers' old ladies don't know me. I know Sasha and Bailey, but only because they both grew up in the club. Though Bailey isn't an old lady anymore. She's with some guy named Zeke, who is the middle son of Anthony fucking Fraser—a big shot mobster.

Nox moves around the front of a large black four-by-four and gets into the driver's seat. I climb into the passenger seat, not sure if I even remember how to drive. It's been so long. I hope I can still ride. I don't want to look like a wet-behind-the-ears prospect, wobbling all over the road.

"Everyone is at the clubhouse waiting for you," he says as I pull the door closed and tug my seatbelt on.

I can't stop grinning. It'll be good to see everyone. I've missed my brothers.

"What about my girl? Where's she at?"

He smirks. "Gasket and Pleck gave her a tune-up. Your bike is waiting for you as soon as you're ready."

The thought of hitting the open road again fills me with a calm I didn't know I needed. I've missed riding so much. Whenever my head was full, or I was feeling stressed, I'd ride. I couldn't do that in jail. I had to find other releases for my stress, my tension. I can't wait to get back out there.

Nox starts the car up and starts the journey back across London to the clubhouse. My gaze is everywhere, taking in all the sights as we pass them. I can't get over how much things have changed over the years. It's like I'm a stranger.

As we get closer to the clubhouse, I start to feel a little tendril of fear trickling through the excitement. What if shit's changed too much? What if I can't slip back into normal life? What if the monsters inside me have taken too much from me, chipped away at my sense of self?

I concentrate on taking steadying breaths. This shit is going to be harder than I imagined. I thought I'd get out of jail and just slot straight into normal life, but I don't think it's going to be that easy. I feel like a boat, blown off course in stormy waters.

When we drive through the compound gates, past the chain-link perimeter fence, my stomach feels uneasy. I jiggle my leg as I peer through the windscreen, taking a moment to study the building. Nothing has changed in the time I've been gone. There are still rows of bikes outside the front entrance, and the same banner still hangs over the doorway with the Sons' insignia staring back at me. The paintwork looks tired, but it's all the same. Relief floods me. It eases some of the pressure crushing my chest.

I spent so many nights here, shooting the shit with the

lads or balls deep inside a bunny that it's like a second home to me.

Fuck, it seems like another lifetime ago.

I give Nox my focus as he tugs up the handbrake and turns to me. The lift of his lips has me mirroring him, even though my nerves are on edge.

"You ready?"

I know what he's asking. Do I need a minute to get my shit locked down? I appreciate it. I'm feeling overwhelmed as hell right now, but I'll never admit that.

"Yeah, brother. I'm ready."

I take a steadying breath and climb out of the car at the same time as Nox.

I can hear the music coming from inside already, the bass a dull thud. I follow Nox through the doors and out of the chilly mid-afternoon air.

As we approach the common room doors, I take a breath. I can do this.

Nox steps in first, and I follow on his heels to raucous yells and whoops. My gaze scans the room quickly, seeing faces of men closer than blood to me, but before I get a good look, I'm surrounded, brothers wanting to embrace me and welcome me home. Hands on me feel odd, uncomfortable. I never let anyone touch me inside. They would die and they knew it. Here, I have to control the urge to put men I consider family on the ground.

"Move out of the way, fuckers," Ravage booms over the music. My eyes snap up as my brothers move out of the way to let him through.

I saw Prez just over a month ago during a visit, but he seems somehow bigger, more intimidating without a table between us. Even though I know he won't do shit to me, I brace, expecting trouble. Inside, I was always on my guard. I guess that habit's going to be hard to break.

His mouth is tipped up at the corners as he strides towards me, a kutte clutched in his hands.

"Missing something?" He hands it to me, and I take it, feeling the worn leather against my skin. "Put it on," he orders.

I do as I'm told, slipping it over my arms. It fits, not quite as well as it did, but considering how much I've bulked up during my time in prison, it's not as tight as I expected.

Rav grins at me and clamps his hand on my shoulder, squeezing hard enough to bruise.

"Welcome fucking home, Stoker."

Cheers go up again.

A pint glass is shoved in my hand by Daimon, who is smirking at me.

"Fuck, thanks, man."

I raise my glass in a toast before I take a long gulp, relishing the malty taste as it slides down my throat.

Fucking nectar of the gods.

As I move between the crowd, receiving back slaps from men I haven't seen in months, years in some cases, I feel overwhelmed by the number of people welcoming me home.

Dizzy by the sensory overload and needing space, I do my best not to rush from the common room. I need to be alone for just a second to digest this shit. I barely notice Fury, who is sitting at a table with a woman holding his hand. If my head was screwed on right, I would have taken a moment to realise something happened there. Fury used to freak out at being touched.

I don't know how to deal with everything. Inside I was somebody feared, envied, admired. Out here, I'm just another brother, following orders.

I'm nobody.

People aren't scared of me.

They're afraid of the patch.

How do I find my place again?

My head spins and my heart hammers as I push through the doors and sag against the wall. I feel like I'm unravelling.

"Shit!"

"You okay?" Nox has followed me out and is looking at me like I might lose my mind. I might. I'm edgy, uncertain, and overwhelmed.

"I just need a second," I admit, scraping my fingers through my hair. I need more than a second.

Nox considers me for a moment.

"Understand," he says. "Titch left you a present in the room down the hallway. She's yours as long as you want her. Might be enough to take the edge off, brother."

He doesn't say anything else and walks back into the common area, the music loud for a second as the door opens before fading back to a duller pitch.

Titch got me a club bunny? Fuck, my dick sits up at that. It's been so long since I last got laid. I'm not sure if I remember how to work my cock anymore.

I consider going outside into the night air to clear my head, but my feet move towards the room. My cock might be rusty, but it's not broken, and the thought of strings-free sex is fucking appealing.

I steal into the room Nox told me about, slowly turning the handle and step into the room.

The woman is lying on the bed, her black leather dress rucked up her thighs, barely hiding her pussy from view. Her makeup is heavy but not tacky but what surprises me is the shit-kicker knee-high boots at the side of the bed. Bunnies are usually more about the skyscraper-high heels.

She's beautiful, with luscious dark hair and bright red lipstick on her pouty lips—lips that beg to be kissed.

I step closer to her, watching the way the bedside lamp bounces the light off her perfect features, and my cock starts to stir in my jeans. Titch did well. This woman is gorgeous and so different from the other bunnies that I've seen tonight. There's nothing fake or plastic about this woman. She's all soft curves.

I move to the side of the bed and sink onto the edge of it. I gently nudge her. I'm eager to get this party started. Hopefully, I can lose myself for a while in her sweet pussy.

"Sweetheart, wake up."

She doesn't open her eyes immediately, but I can see how she tries to pull herself out of the sleep fog, her eyes flickering open. They drift up and find my face. For a moment, I see her confusion.

Then she screams.

2

LAYLA

AN HOUR EARLIER...

I rub at my temples as the pain starts to pound. The music blearing out of the speaker behind the bar is not helping. The clubhouse is heaving tonight. This isn't my first club party, but it's the first one I've been to for a brother getting out of prison. I had no idea they even celebrated this kind of thing, but these guys use any excuse to have a shindig.

Briella, my best friend, is standing next to me with a glass of soda in her hand. She's been tee total for the past five years, ever since she got with Daimon.

I was worried about her dating the Treasurer of the Untamed Sons Motorcycle Club, but honestly, he's been a rock for her. His support enabled her to come out of some fairly dark places she was trapped in. That story isn't mine to tell, but it always makes me feel a wave of anger when I think about what she suffered.

It's good to see her happy.

Over the years that I've been friends with Brie, I've been to a lot of club events—mostly club cookouts and birthday parties—but tonight has been something else. None of the kids are here, unlike at the monthly family day I usually go to, and the atmosphere is completely different without them. I like to party. I'm pretty much known for it, but this is wild even by my standards.

I'm used to seeing shit I can't bleach from my brain, but the atmosphere tonight is different.

I can't put my finger on it.

I rub at my temples again as a blast of pain attacks my brain.

"You're getting a migraine," Brie says.

Trust her to recognise the symptoms.

We lived together for a while before she moved in with her man, so she's seen me suffer through my share of migraines before. This one has been brewing all day, and I thought if I took my meds, it might die down, but it doesn't seem like it's going to. I'm starting to feel nauseous and a little dizzy. It's not alcohol related. I no longer drink when I'm with Briella. Not because I think she'll succumb to temptation and drink again, but I want to show my support. Over the years, it's just kind of stuck, and I don't do it from habit now.

"Yeah, shitty timing. Sorry, Brie."

She shakes her head. "Don't apologise. You can't help it. You need to go home?"

I glance around the room. The party is in full swing. There are a few club bunnies fucking and sucking their way around the brothers. Old ladies are gathered in packs, trying to ignore the shit going on around them. Maybe they can zone it out—years of practice, I guess.

I see the guy who the party is in honour of.

He's got one tattoo down his right arm, a wash of colours and shapes like an artist's canvas, and his face is covered with hair that needs a trim. I doubt he got much chance to do that inside. His kutte, which Ravage gave back to him a little while ago, looks a little small around the arm holes as if he bulked out inside. His tee is clinging to the contours of his body. I can't stop my gaze from drifting to his thick biceps and veiny forearms.

Stoker.

What kind of name is that?

All these men have weird as hell names. I've come to accept it, but Stoker seems like it could be a surname, maybe.

I don't know him. I wasn't around before he got locked up and I'm not that involved with the club to have been told about him. A week ago was the first time I heard his name mentioned. Brie doesn't know him either. He was locked up before she came into the club.

I don't know what he did to get locked up—no one is talking about it. Honestly, I think ignorance is bliss in this life. It's better not knowing these things.

"No, I'm not going home." If I go home, Brie will want to come with me, and I'm not dragging her out of this party. Not when she looks relaxed and like she's having fun. She deserves that.

Daimon is across the room with Levi, Titch, and some guy called Cage. I notice he keeps glancing in her direction. I smirk. Even after all this time, he can't keep his gaze off her.

"Do you want to lie down for a bit? It might help."

That sounds like a good idea. Sleep might just be enough to stop it from progressing into a full-blown migraine with all the fun side effects that brings.

"Would that be okay?"

She signals over Daimon, who crosses the room instantly. She explains what is going on and that I need to lie down for a bit.

"There's a room at the end of the hall you can use," he says. "No one will bother you."

I slide my glass onto the bar, murmuring a thank you, and

head to the room. As I move up the corridor, I feel like I'm somewhere I shouldn't be, even though I was given permission. My heart starts to beat a little faster as I go towards the room.

It's quieter down this end of the building, and I'm glad Brie suggested this because my head is starting to pound.

The room I was directed to is small, but there's a bed in the middle of the floor and not a lot else—some shabby drawers and a nightstand. I move to the adjacent bathroom and switch the light on, leaving the door open just enough to cast a glow over the room. I'm not scared of the dark, but waking up somewhere strange in the dark might be a little disorienting.

I step over to the bed and drop my hands to my hips. Considering how sex-crazed these people are, I'm not getting under the blankets. God knows what sort of petri dish of bacteria lies on those sheets.

Yuck.

I pull my boots off, sticking them at the side of the bed, and crawl on top of the duvet, which actually smells fresh, as if it was recently washed. That eases some of the tension in me, though I wonder who the hell does the laundry in this place. The thought of one of the brothers loading the machine makes me want to laugh.

I snuggle into the pillows, close my eyes and let myself drift.

I don't know how long I sleep, but I'm dragged awake as I become aware of a presence in the room. Slowly, I open my eyes and see there's a figure sitting on the edge of the bed.

It's surprise more than fear that makes the scream wrench out of my throat as I jack-knife up into a sitting position. I take him in with a fleeting glance, trying to note everything at once. All I see is the black leather kutte, tattoos, dark hair, and a beard.

It's Stoker.

The man who just got released from jail.

Why the hell is he sitting on the edge of the bed?

I pull a pillow over my lap as if it can offer me protection.

"Fuck, didn't mean to startle you, darlin'." He holds his hands up in supplication as if that will calm me.

The hand not clutching the pillow goes to my sternum, trying to stop my heart from pounding out of my chest.

"It's okay." I wave him off, trying to calm my pulse.

His gaze crawls over my face before lingering on my tits for a moment longer than he should. I arch a brow at him as he brings his attention back to my face.

He scans my face. His brows are drawn together. "You're not what I was expecting," he admits.

I'm not sure why, but his words sting. What was he expecting? I know I'm not curvy like a lot of the women here tonight. I have a slight body with a slim waist. I've learnt to love the frame I have, and I do love it, so his words fucking grate on my nerves.

"You're not what I was expecting either," I fire back, irritation making my tone angry.

"Retract the claws, kitten. I meant you're better than that."

He surprises the hell out of me by reaching out and stroking his fingers down my cheek. I freeze solid like a block of ice. I'm not averse to him touching me—I mean, the man is a snack—but I don't know him, and this feels intimate.

"What are you doing?" I demand, my voice croaky.

Has he lost his mind? Did prison destroy it?

My gaze drifts to his lips as his tongue darts out to wet them. They are full and perfect for kissing. I shouldn't be thinking about that, but I can't stop the thought from drifting across my mind.

"You're fucking pretty," he tells me. "More than pretty. You're gorgeous."

His strong hand cups the back of my head, forcing me closer to his mouth. I can feel his hot breath against my skin, the smell of beer faintly tingeing the air. My chest starts to heave as I meet his gaze, our eyes like magnets.

I've never had such a visceral reaction to a man before. I've never wanted more without knowing more, but with him, I don't care about that shit.

Without warning, he pulls me towards him and his hold on my head is so firm, I have no choice but to go.

Then he presses his mouth unapologetically to mine.

He's kissing me.

The man who just got released from prison is *kissing* me.

I should push him away. I should tell him no, but instead, I melt into his arms. My blood heats and my skin tingles. Every inch of my body feels like it's on fire. I've never been kissed like this. It's hot and heavy and demanding.

And I fucking love it.

For someone who has been locked up away from society for as long as he has, he can sure as fuck use that mouth of his. I tremble, and it's a good thing I'm sitting in the bed, or I might lose my footing. I feel weak, shaky. I lean into him as he drags my fingers closer.

His tongue slides into my mouth, and that breaks through my thoughts. This isn't right.

I place a hand on his chest and push him back. His lips unglue from mine, and I miss his touch instantly. I should have kept taking from him.

He peers into my face, and I wonder if my lips look as swollen as his. Then his mouth curls into a sneer that makes my stomach twist.

"Sweetheart, if you don't want to do this, just say the word. Ain't into forcing a bitch to do anything."

His words and the sharpness of his tone have me drawing my brows together. What the hell? The change in direction gives me whiplash.

"Excuse me?"

He gets up from the bed and paces the floor, his fingers tearing through his hair. I can see the genuine annoyance in him as he does.

"Nox said you were fucking waiting for me."

He did? Why would he say that? "Well, I wasn't." I huff before scrambling back out of the other side of the bed, putting some distance—and the mattress—between us. I can't think after that kiss. I need space. "Believe me, no one in their right mind would be waiting for someone as arrogant as you are."

I don't know what possesses me to say it. These men are dangerous. Clearly, Stoker falls into that same category. The man went to prison—for *years*. He's not someone to mess with. Yet my stupid mouth won't stop running. It's almost like I have a death wish.

"Didn't realise they let snatch answer back," he snarls.

I roll my eyes at his crudeness. If he's looking to shock me with his words, he's not going to succeed. I'm not easily shocked. "I'm *not* snatch."

"What are you doing here then?"

"Well, I was sleeping!" At least my migraine seems to have settled down, though this guy seems like he has the ability to induce a whole new headache.

He stares at me like I've grown two heads.

"Sleeping?"

"I had a migraine. Brie told me to come and lay down."

"Brie . . . Briella—Daimon's old lady? The fuck she got to do with this?"

"She's the one who suggested I sleep. Then Daimon said I could use the room at the end of the hall—"

He holds a hand up, and I fall silent. "You ain't a bunny?"

He thinks I'm a fucking bunny? Is he crazy? I peer down at my leather dress and I can understand why he might think that.

I give him my best death glare. It could melt glaciers. "I'm not a whore."

He considers me for a moment. "What's your name?"

"Layla."

"You're friends with Briella?"

"Best friends." I don't know why I say that. It makes me sound ten. Inwardly, I cringe.

He doesn't seem to care, though. He's just staring at me intently. I want to squirm under his scrutiny, but I force my body to stay still.

"Thought you were a bunny Titch set me up with."

"I'm sorry to disappoint."

"You haven't."

His words make warmth spread through me. These men are nothing if not forward, and I know if he says it, he means it.

"Your old man around?"

"I don't have one."

"How ain't you been snapped up?"

Heat pools in my belly at his words. "You're a smooth talker for someone who just got out of prison."

His eyes get a little sad, a little distant as he sinks onto the edge of the bed. "Got a lot of time to make up. Missed a lot of shit I regret."

I move around the bed and perch next to him. "You have the opportunity to do that."

He glances at me. "Can't get time back, Layla. Once it's gone, it's gone. Slips through your fingers like sand. Most of us never realise how precious time is until you wake up one day and realise you lost half your life."

I shouldn't ask it, but curiosity gets the better of me. "What were you inside for?"

"Doesn't matter now."

I don't push him. If he doesn't want to tell me, I'm not going to make him. I know better than to poke a biker anyway. I'm not crazy, and while I trust the other brothers, I don't know this guy, and that makes me wary. Prison could have changed him—likely it did. He might not be the same Stoker they remember. He might not even recognise the man he's become himself.

All I know is when he kissed me, I wanted more.

It's been a long time since a man last kissed me with such desperation, such longing. It is a heady feeling, one I want to recapture.

I shouldn't do it, but I turn to face him, staring into those dark eyes as if they hold all the answers.

I don't know if it's the fuzziness from the aftermath of my migraine that makes all my inhibitions disappear, but I don't think. I press my mouth to his.

He doesn't hesitate to kiss me back. His fingers thread into my hair, so he can pull me closer, deepen the kiss. His tongue explores my mouth, taking everything I offer and more.

My body feels warm heated and between my legs throbs. I want him to touch me. I want to feel him against me. His hand moves to my left tit and he slips it down the front of my dress so he can knead it. I can't stop the moan that leaves my mouth as he rolls my nipple between his finger and thumb.

It's like that movement has a direct line to my pussy, and everything down there throbs. I throw my head back and pant as his mouth sucks up around my neck, leaving marks, no doubt. I should care about that, but I can't bring myself to. All I can focus on is the sensations of his mouth and hands on me.

He pushes me back onto the bed, and I go down on my back as he comes down on top of me. His hard-on pressing through his jeans is an unmistakable presence as it pushes against my core. Fuck, I want it inside me and I widen my thighs to give him better access to my pussy.

"Fuck me," I moan.

He laughs. "Impatient little thing, aren't you?"

"You're the one who hasn't been laid in years. Thought you'd be more wham bam."

He shakes his head before he kisses me. "Ain't a selfish prick in bed, baby."

He moves down the bed and pushes my dress up. The leather is stiff, and his hands are forceful on my skin as he exposes between my legs. My underwear is pulled down my legs, leaving my pussy on display to him.

I don't have a chance to feel embarrassed at sharing myself with a stranger because his tongue flattens against my sex, and my hips arch off the bed. Fuck, that feels so good.

He licks and laps at my clit as his fingers enter me. The dual sensation of being licked and finger-fucked makes my whole body tremble. I have a healthy sex life and a string of one-night stands behind me, but this is something else entirely. There's a connection between us I didn't expect. I keep my eyes locked on the top of his head as he continues to lick and suck at my most sensitive spot. His tongue is like magic, and I can barely draw in a breath as my pussy starts to pulse. I'm going to come. This is going to be fast.

He continues to piston his fingers in and out of me as he licks me. I'm unravelling fast and I orgasm around him, my head thrown back, the muscles of my neck taut as I come harder than I have in years.

"Fuck!" I drape my arm over my face as I try to control my breathing.

"Birth control."

"Condom," I gasp. My migraines mean I can't take certain pills. I could go on something else, but I tend to just rely on condoms.

I lay trying to control my pounding heart as he moves to the drawer at the side of the bed. He finds a condom in there, which should concern me. Is this room just a sex room?

I watch him as he pushes down his jeans and his cock is freed. It's long, thick, and veiny. Fuck, he's going to be an unforgettable presence inside me.

I let my legs fall open wider, readying for him as he opens the packet and rolls it down his shaft. I feel him at my entrance, his dick thick as he rubs through my folds.

"Ready?" he asks.

I nod, and he pushes roughly inside me. I can't stop the gasp of pain that escapes my mouth. My pussy burns at the intrusion as he stretches me. God, he's big, and I have to resist the urge to tense around him. I try to relax as he gets himself seated inside me, but all I can focus on is the feel of him. I cling to his shoulders, my nails digging into the skin.

He brushes my hair off my face, a move at odds with the roughness he just exerted. Then he starts to move.

The pinch of pain melts into pleasure after a few thrusts, and I start to feel the familiar build of excitement in my pussy as he moves in and out of me.

He watches my face intently as I pant through each pump of his hips. He's not gentle as his hands roam my breasts, touching, pinching. I don't want soft. I want hard and fast, and that's what he gives me.

Eventually, he grabs my wrists and holds them over my head, keeping me from moving, and the loss of control has me coming apart. My hips twitch as I go over the edge, and he follows me a moment later, spunking into the condom.

He collapses onto me, and for a moment, neither of us speaks as we try to control our breathing.

3

STOKER

I'M NOT the kissing and cuddling type, so part of me is relieved when Layla comes out of the bathroom after cleaning up and instantly pulls her dress back on.

Another part of me fucking hates that she does.

I don't say anything. Instead, I watch as she slides her dress up her hips, the leather clinging to her in all the right places. She's fucking gorgeous with all that dark hair spilling over her shoulders and those pert tits with dark nipples that beg to be sucked on. I want to do more to her. I want to fuck her until she's crying my name but getting too close is a bad idea.

She has to go.

I don't want to feel anything, and right now, all that is rushing through my veins is hope.

That's dangerous.

Hope can change a man, can destroy him too.

I just left a hopeless place. I'm not looking to revisit rock bottom.

So nothing can happen here.

She's not mine, and I'm not hers. I need space, time to

breathe and decompress from what's happened today. I'm still reeling from my newfound freedom.

It's that which makes my tongue glued to the roof of my mouth.

I'm a dick, I know, but clearly, she's not keen on the idea of sticking around either. I have to admit that offends me. Was it that bad she needs to flee like she has a rocket up her arse?

She sits on the edge of the bed to put her boots on. Shit kickers, knee-high and sexy as fuck. They shouldn't be, but they are. I'm used to bitches in stilettos and fuck-me boots. Layla's footwear says she's girly, but she'll kick me in the balls if I overstep.

I like that more than I should.

"So, that was fun," she says as she laces her boots. "It definitely helped with the migraine."

"Glad to have been of service," I mutter, sounding as bitter as I feel.

Even though I know this is for the best, I can't help but feel regret. Another time, another place, maybe we could have been more, but right now, my only focus is on getting back into things with the club and sorting my life back out.

I don't need the complications of a relationship. I had enough of people telling me what to do in jail. Don't need a ball and chain on the outside.

My problem is the chemistry between us. It flows like an electrical current, and when I was with her, I felt light. At ease in a way I never have before. That was a heady relief and an addictive feeling.

Her gaze drifts in my direction and she curves her mouth into a smirk. "We should do that again sometime."

"Yeah," I agree.

"Don't know who you were waiting for, but I'm happy she never showed up."

Me too.

Whichever bunny would have come through those doors wouldn't have been better than what I had. Layla is beautiful, good in bed, and fuck, I want more. I don't want her to leave.

"You have to go?"

She gives me a look. "I think that's for the best, don't you?"

No.

"Yeah."

She pushes to her feet, now fully dressed, and smooths the leather down her body. I watch as she stalks towards me, a beautiful gazelle offering herself to the lion. She rolls to the balls of her feet and kisses my cheek.

"See you around, Stoker."

I don't move as she leaves the room, but my stomach feels heavy, leaden.

I want to put my fist through the wall, but instead, I clean myself up and head back to the party. The room is loud, a few brothers drunk already weaving through the crush of people in the room. I peer around, trying to spot Layla, but there's no sign of her. If she came back to the main common room, she sure as fuck didn't stay.

With a heavy sigh, I make a beeline for the bar and get a drink from Tommy, one of the prospects. I down the amber coloured liquid in one flick of a wrist, enjoying the burn as it moves down my throat.

"Where'd you go, brother?" Titch asks as he sidles up next to me. He smirks as he says, "You get my gift."

I don't answer that question. Instead, I say, "What do you know about Layla?"

I can't resist asking. I need to know everything I can about her.

"She's Brie's bestie. She's good people." He grins. "You like her?"

"I fucked her," I admit.

I don't know why I do, but I can't stop my mouth from running. Titch's grin grows. "Fuck, brother. You move fast."

"Got a lot of time to make up." Tommy places another drink in front of me, but this one, I sip. Titch takes the other glass.

"Ain't that the truth." He raises the pint in salute. "Welcome home, Stoker."

THE NEXT WEEK passes in a blur of activity. Getting back into my stride takes longer than I would like. It isn't easy to just slot back into the club. Things have changed. There're new brothers, new old ladies, familiar faces who have gone, left, been killed, or got themselves arrested. There's more of a family atmosphere than there ever was previously.

Everyone has kids—apart from Daimon and Brie, but they're starting to think about growing their family. The clubhouse is like a fucking crèche some days, with kids running around screaming and playing with bikers. I don't mind them, but it's not the world I left behind. This is something else.

Rav eases me back into shit, putting me to work in the garage with Gasket and Pleck. I knew the brothers before I got locked up and I like both men, though Pleck can be a lazy cunt at times. He spends more time flirting with the female customers than working.

Pleck has to show me how to fix the newer cars up. They have fancy as fuck electronics they never had in the past. I feel out of my fucking depth.

The only thing that keeps me going through this time is Layla. She's in my fucking mind more than she should be, haunting my steps. I want to see her again, the need a persistent itch that I need to scratch. But it's not a good idea, and she doesn't hang around the clubhouse like Brie and the other old ladies anyway, so the opportunity to see her doesn't present. As far as I can find out, Layla only comes to a few special occasions. It was the luck of the draw she was here for my welcome home party.

The more I think about that fact, the more I think we were just meant to fucking be, and that's dangerous. I'm not ready for more, yet I can't get her out of my head. I have to fix my own head first, but I'm drawn to Layla in ways I can't even explain.

"What's up with your mug?" Gasket asks from under the hood of the car. He's set me up under an older model Ford that predates all the computer shit. That stuff just fucking bamboozles me.

"Ain't fuck all wrong with me," I snap out.

I know I'm being a dick. I've been on fucking edge all day. Even though it's been a week since I came home, I still feel like a fucking outsider. I still don't fit with this place. The brothers have welcomed me back with open arms, so I know the issue is with me, not them, but fuck, I can't get around it. I don't belong here. The kutte hanging in the cloakroom of the garage doesn't feel like mine. I feel wrong. Out of fucking sorts. I'm struggling. Prison was hell, but there was a routine to it that I understood. I don't get this shit. The freedom to do what I want is bizarre. I'm used to being told what to do and when to do it, even down to when I can shower. I have to relearn autonomy.

Gasket goes back to what he's doing while I toss down the wrench and stride out of the garage. I need air, space to breathe. I always feel like there are fingers at my neck, trying to suffocate me, trying to choke the life out of me.

My fingers go to the back of my neck and I resist the urge to roar my frustration into the sky.

That's when I see her.

Layla.

She's on the clubhouse compound, climbing out of Briella's car. Brie gets out, too, laughing at something Layla says.

I don't think. I cross the garage parking area and go to the gate that separates the business from the clubhouse. As I step through it, she sees me. I'm not sure if it's the clanging of the metal against metal that alerts her to my presence or something else, but her eyes go over the roof of the car and lock onto mine.

I don't stop moving towards her as she goes around the front of the bonnet and waits for me to reach her. Brie glances between us both as I approach, and while she's not wary, she is curious.

"Hey, big guy."

Fuck, Layla sounds angelic, like a good girl wrapped in devilish packaging. She's wearing a tiny vest top and cut-off jean shorts that ride up her thighs, showing an expanse of flesh that makes my mouth fucking water. Memories of her beneath me as I pounded into her assault me, and I want to take her again. I want to push her against the car and rub against her. If Briella wasn't here, I would.

"Where've you been?" My words sound accusatory, even though I don't mean them to. Why do I care where the fuck she's been? Ain't her old man. Ain't nothing to her.

She turns to Brie, her hand resting on her bicep. "Give us a minute, yeah?"

Brie doesn't look sure. She fires me a look that says if I hurt her friend, she'll cut me into pieces, and I believe she would. Even so, she does turn and walk towards the clubhouse, glancing over her shoulder as she reaches the door.

Layla waits for her to get inside before she gives me her attention.

"What we had was fun, right?"

"It was," I agree.

"Happy to do it again, but not if you're going to make this shit into something it's not." Her smile is lopsided as she takes me in. "I don't do relationships, Romeo."

Neither do I, so I don't know why her words fucking piss me off. The last thing I want with her is anything serious.

"Ain't looking for that," I grind out.

She tilts her head to the side, considering me. "What are you looking for then?"

I don't even know.

I force a grin. "All I want from you, sweetheart, is a good time."

"Well, in that case, I have you covered." She leans in and speaks directly into my ear. "Why don't you come to my place tonight? We can pick up where we left off."

It's a tantalising suggestion, one I would be crazy to give up. I want her. I need to feel her beneath me, hear her moans as I slide into that sweet pussy of hers and if it comes with no strings attached . . .

That's what I want, right? No-fuss fucking. No clingy bitches demanding I make them my old lady.

This is the perfect outcome for us both.

Casual sex.

Good sex at that.

She's a great lay.

For now, it's enough.

It has to be. I don't have the head space for more.

"Where do you live?"

She gives me her address and says, "Don't be late."

No fucking chance of that.

I watch her walk the same path Brie took a moment ago, my eyes glued to the pert globes of her arse.

This could be a mistake.

4

LAYLA

No strings sex with a hot as fuck biker is dangerous. I'm dipping my toes into a river of lava, trying to test the temperature, even though I know it will burn me.

I shouldn't entertain this notion with Stoker. The man is a convicted criminal—although that doesn't bother me as much as it probably should. Most of the men I know run in those circles, and even though they indulge in acts that society deems bad, all I see are good, decent men. Don't get me wrong, Ravage and Fury scare the hell out of me, but I know they would do anything to protect their families. I've seen it a number of times in the past.

Stoker is cut from the same cloth. He's a man of action who will do what it takes to protect the club, to protect his brothers and their families. These men are all the same.

They're all intense as fuck when it comes to their women. I don't know how Brie doesn't suffocate under Daimon's possessiveness. I don't want that. As much as I can look at them together and feel a hint of jealousy at what they have, that intensity would make me crackers. I need space to breathe, to be free. I don't trust men, even these men. They usually get their fill and leave. I fully expect Stoker to do the same, which is why I'm not getting attached. He'll walk away in the end, just like all the others.

Mindless sex is the best way.

No feelings involved.

No one can get hurt.

That's just how I like it.

It's why I have a string of one-night stands in my past. I've never had a real relationship, and I don't plan on it.

Yet, Stoker's already getting clingy. I can see it in the way he asked where I'd been. They're not the words of a man who isn't interested. For that reason, I should nip this shit in the bud. I should walk away, but I can't stop wanting him. His need burning through my veins, and that scares me. I don't want to get embedded in his shit. I want to get my rocks off and walk away. I have too much other shit to deal with without adding a possessive biker to the mix.

Yet, I'm sitting on my sofa, my robe wrapped around me, hiding the tiny thong and bra set I'm wearing, waiting for him to turn up. I shaved every inch of my body for this hook-up.

When there's a knock on the door, I push to my feet and fluff my hair a little. I've left it loose around my shoulders.

Before I open the door, I check through the peep hole and see Stoker standing waiting. My mouth begins to dry and between my legs pulses in preparation for what is going to come. The man can fuck, and I can't wait to have him between my legs.

I unlock the door and tug it open. His eyes move from my face to the robe I'm wearing. It's silky and barely covers me. It's sexy as fuck.

"Hey, big guy," I say.

He doesn't hesitate, he pushes me back into the flat, and I

find myself pressed against the wall. He grinds against me, and I wish there wasn't the barrier of clothes between us.

"Do you always answer the door like this?" he demands as he captures my wrists and holds them over my head. My pussy throbs at the friction between our clothes.

"This is all for you, Stoker."

He attacks my mouth, his tongue sliding over the slit in my lips until I part to give him access. My heart is pounding as he presses his hardness against my core. It's not going to be enough. I need him inside me. I need him to fuck me hard and fast. I don't want soft. I don't need gentle from him. I need raw and rough.

He seems like he's going to give me what I want when he releases his hold on me and his hand dips under my robe. He shoves aside my thong and slides his fingers inside me. I widen my stance to give him better access.

My nails dig into his shoulders as he finger-fucks me, all while devouring my mouth still. I can barely draw in air as he claims my mouth like a starving man. He's so intense, so beautifully broken too. I see it in his eyes, the demons that sit beneath the surface, waiting to erupt. Like all his brothers, he sees the world in shades of grey. There's no colour.

My thoughts scatter as he hooks his fingers deeper inside me, and my orgasm builds. I tear my mouth from his as I tip my head back, panting so hard I feel dizzy. He shrugs out of his kutte, tossing it onto the edge of the sofa a few feet away, and drags his tee over his head.

He has a good body, and my hands trace the contours of his muscles as his fingers go back inside me. Every thrust seems to go deeper, and I need more. Fingers aren't going to cut it. I need his cock.

"Fuck me, Stoker," I beg.

He doesn't need telling twice. He unbuttons his jeans and

shoves them down his thighs. I tug my robe open, giving him an eye full of my lace-covered bra.

"This is fucking pretty, sweetheart," he mutters. "You wear this for me?"

I nod, pulling my bottom lip between my teeth. He's so hot it should be illegal.

His hand gropes at my breast before slipping under the cup and freeing me from the material. He dips his head and takes a nipple in his mouth, laving around the bud and sucking it hard enough to make it a hard bud. I slide my fingers into his hair, needing to draw him closer as he continues to lick at me. Fuck, it's like my tits have a direct line to my pussy because everything down there is contracting and pulsating.

"Stoker..."

"Going to fuck you now, sweetheart," he tells me.

I nod. "Please."

He pushes his jeans the rest of the way down, stripping out of them and releasing his cock. I stare at the thick length, waiting as he tugs a condom free of his wallet and rolls it down his shaft.

His eyes meet mine before he pulls me against him. I feel him line up his dick with my pussy, and then he slams into me. I moan instantly at the fullness of him. That feels so good. I cling to his shoulders as he lifts one of my legs so he can fuck me deeper.

Every thrust pushes me closer to the edge. As with the first time, it's dirty, raw, and hard. There's not an ounce of gentleness from him. He fucks me against the wall like an animal, and I come so hard I see stars.

He follows me over the edge a moment later. I stare into his eyes as he comes into the condom, and there's no denying the connection between us. It zings between us, electric.

He releases his hold on me, and I put my foot back on the carpet.

"Fuck," he mutters, his forehead pressing to mine.

"You want to go again?" I grin.

Stoker shakes his head. "I'm going to need a minute here, Layla."

"Well, while you take that minute, why don't we go somewhere a little more comfortable?"

I take his hand and lead him into the bedroom. His eyes are everywhere as he takes in my space. It's not overly girly, though it is decorated in hot pink and black. I have fairy lights around my bed, something I probably shouldn't have at twenty-five years old, but this is who I am.

I crawl onto the bed and pat the space next to me for him to join. He does. His cock is softening now, and I want to arouse him again, but instead, I lean my head on the pillows and look at him.

"You don't have to answer this, but what did you do to get locked up for so long?"

"Does it matter?"

I sigh. "I suppose not."

"We fuck. We don't need to know each other."

His words don't sting, though they should. We both know what we're in this for and what we're getting out of it. I have no intention of being tied down, and neither does he.

"You aren't even the slightest bit curious about me?"

"Layla." He says my name softly.

I hold my hands up. "I'm not asking you to fucking marry me, Stoker."

"Ain't ready for more than what we're doing."

"I'm not looking for more either. Relax. You're safe." I roll my eyes. "I'm not girlfriend material."

He takes this in without a word before he says, "I got caught with a gun. They charged me with possession of firearms with intent to cause fear of violence or some shit. I got the toughest sentence they could because of my club links. Ten years, out in nine. It was an eternity."

My heart contracts painfully in my chest. "I'm sorry."

He shrugs my sympathy off. "I knew better than to have one on me, but what do you do when all your enemies carry too? You got to protect yourself. I had to protect my brothers, my prez."

I understand why he'd feel the need to carry, but he paid a high price for it. Better than losing his life, though.

"That's unfair."

"The system ain't fair, sweetheart, but I knew the score, took the risk. Paid for it."

Nine years of his life were gone in the blink of an eye. It makes my heart hurt for him. Years he could have been building a life for himself, having a family, experiences. He must be in his mid to late thirties now, which means he would have gone inside when he was around my age. I can't imagine how that must have felt, staring down the barrel of a loaded gun and waiting for a judge to toss your life on the scrap pile. I can tell he's not slotted back into life easily. He has this air about him that says he's not comfortable in his life, that he's not at ease. He's an outsider looking in, and even though his brothers have no doubt welcomed him home, adjusting to being home is going to take some time. Maybe it'll never happen.

He's got secrets.

We all have.

Even I have them. I keep my friends, my family in the dark about the worst parts of my life. Locked in a cell or locked into a life you despise—it's never been easy. After Briella moved out of the flat to live with Daimon, my life changed, and not for the better. I didn't begrudge my friend all the goodness she got. Brie deserved it and more, but over the past four years, my life has completely spiralled out of control. I'm out of control. I fuck at random. I take strangers home with me. I drink too much and I take drugs to stop my head from spinning for just a few hours. I loved the party life —at least I did until Mitchell showed me the darker side of that world.

Mitchell.

Fuck.

I hate myself for thinking his name. He's like the devil. Speak his name and he'll appear.

I'd lost hold of everything because of Mitchell. This here and now with Stoker is one of the first things I've had control over lately.

My phone starts to vibrate on the bedside table. I lean over and grab it, and my heart sinks as I see the name on the screen. Fuck, thinking about that bastard really did conjure him. It's not surprising, though, that he'd be calling right now. He's left me alone for a week. I thought he was done with me, but clearly, that's not the case.

I scramble to get out of the bed, but Stoker grabs my wrist. "Where're you going?"

"I have to take this."

He must see something in my face or maybe in my tone because he releases his hold on me.

I move into the bathroom and close the door behind me, sinking against the back of it as I stare at the name. Fuck, fuck, fuck. What the hell does he want?

I quickly turn the taps on, and once the water is running, I answer the call.

"Hey."

"The fuck took you so long to answer?" Mitchell demands, his tone abrasive, like acid eating through metal.

"I was asleep." The lie falls so easily from my lips. I hate that it does. I'm not this person. I'm not a liar. I know too much about lying and the damage it causes. I'd seen it with Briella and her alcoholism.

"I need you here."

Now? Fuck, Stoker is still lying in my bed. How do I explain kicking his arse out of my flat, as if what we did was nothing?

"I'm kind of busy."

"Wasn't asking, bitch. You ain't here in an hour. I'll come get you. If I have to do that, I'm going to be pissed."

The phone goes dead. I close my eyes as I lean against the basin. Fuck.

A hammering on the door makes me squeal.

"Layla?" Stoker sounds annoyed, and I don't blame him. I just upped and left halfway through a conversation.

"I'll . . . I'll be out in a second."

I place my phone on the edge of the sink and splash some water on my face. It doesn't clear the panic from my belly. Nothing can do that. Why the fuck does Mitchell want to see me now?

I tug my bottom lip between my fingers as I contemplate my next move.

"Layla." Stoker's impatience shines through his words.

I snag my phone and open the door. Stoker is leaning against the top of the frame, his arms stretched over his head. He's looking at me as if he's waiting for answers. I duck under his arm and move into the bedroom.

"What the fuck was that about?" he demands.

"Nothing."

"I know a thing about lies and liars to know you're feeding me shit right now."

His tone annoys me. He's not my lover. He doesn't get to ask questions. "Does it matter? It was private." I go to the chest of drawers and pull out a clean pair of jeans. I step into them before I search around for my bra.

"You get a call and run out?"

"I have shit to do," I snap, finally losing my temper. "I don't have time or the will to hold your fucking hand, Stoker."

He grabs my wrist, stopping me. "Ain't about that. You look fucking freaked. What's going on?"

"Nothing is going on." I drag my arm free. "I need to go. If you're staying, stay. If not, make sure the door latches when you leave."

I snag my boots off the floor and rush into the living room to stuff my feet inside them. If I'm late, Mitchell will follow through on his threat, and an altercation with him is the last fucking thing I need.

"Babe." I glance up at Stoker standing in the doorway. He's pulled his jeans on though they are unbuttoned, revealing that tantalising hint of what lies beneath the denim.

I try not to think about his cock, about how much I want it again, nor do I think about how much I like him calling me "babe". I can't. I shouldn't be pulling Stoker into my shit. So far, I've been careful about keeping the club out of my business, and I intend to keep it that way.

"I have to go." There's regret in my voice. So much regret but keeping Mitchell waiting is not a good idea. He's not a patient man.

I step over to Stoker and roll to my toes so I can capture his mouth. He kisses me back so gently, so at odds with the shit that spews from his mouth. He says he doesn't want commitment, but this kiss says something different. It's so intimate it makes my toes curl into my boots.

"I have to go," I repeat.

He doesn't say a word as I go to the front door and step through it. Only once I'm away from his gaze do I let the fear slide onto my face.

I grab a black cab from outside my building, though it

takes me a few minutes for one to pass, and head across town to the territory of the Crimson Vipers. My foot jiggles as the cab passes familiar London landmarks. This isn't going to end well.

The car stops outside the Vipers' club. I quickly shove a tenner at the driver and climb out of the vehicle. Keeping Mitchell waiting is not a good idea, and he's already waited long enough.

I head for the doors of the club. One of Mitchell's goons is standing outside, a silent sentinel. I recognise him, but I don't know his name. I don't want to either. The less I know, the better.

He opens the door for me, and I step into the darkened building. The bar runs the length of the room, and there are booths and tables scattered around the large space. The decor is classy, dark but modern. I step further into the room, my heart starting to pound. What the hell is this shit about? Why does Mitchell suddenly want to see me?

I take two steps, and then a hand grabs the back of my neck. I freeze at the unyielding hold, fingers bruising my skin. I know instantly who it is.

Mitchell.

He moves to my ear, his breath warm against my skin.

"Where the fuck have you been?"

This isn't like when Stoker asked. This is different. There's menace in his voice: demand and anger. I can't brush Mitchell off.

"If you needed me, you only had to call."

"Shouldn't need to fucking call. You should just be here."

His fingers slide to the apex between my legs, a place where Stoker touched me with such reverence just a few hours ago. Mitchell's touch is nothing like his. It's hard, rough. Aggressive. He grabs my hair and drags my head back, so I'm nearly looking at the ceiling. "You belong to me. I own you. Don't ever forget it."

I want to tell him to go fuck himself, but fear keeps my tongue glued to the roof of my mouth. Mitchell isn't someone to mess with. I should have realised that before I got involved in his world. I should have seen the danger. I've been around dangerous men for years, but by the time I realised he was a devil, I was already shackled to him.

He continues to rub me through my clothes, his other hand fisted in my hair still, and I whimper. I hate myself for getting turned on by it. What kind of person does that make me? I let a monster touch me, and I respond to it.

"Mitchell, stop." The words rip out of me.

He doesn't. He never does.

Instead, he pushes me against the bar, my tits pressing against the wood and bends me over, his hand pressing against my neck, his hardness against my arse.

"You don't give the fucking orders. You're mine, bitch. I own you. Don't you fucking forget it."

I swallow back bile. I never wanted to be his. Defiance wars with reason, as I want to tell him to fuck off, but sense keeps me silent.

Despite my denials, I have no doubt he owns me completely. I'm Mitchell's fuck toy, his marionette that he makes dance however he wants to. I hate him for that. I hate that I ever let him into my life. My fucking partying ways brought this crap into my life and now I'm trapped. I'll always be trapped.

Which means I have to end things with Stoker.

I won't drag him into my mess. I won't bring the club into my shit either, even though I know they would help to pull me out of this quicksand I'm sinking in.

The problem is, I don't want to end things.

I like spending time with Stoker. We're both two sides of

the same coin. Both broken and damaged in ways that make us messy.

Mitchell flips me around, so I'm facing him. As always, the handsomeness of his face distracts me from the darkness behind his eyes. He's a beautiful man. It was why I was first attracted to him, why I pursued him. If I knew then what I know now, I would have run.

Now, I'm a fly caught in a spider's web, waiting to be eaten.

He glares at me, his eyes blazing fire. "I'm going to ask you this once, and you'd better not lie."

"Okay."

"Who's the fucker who came to your flat?"

Cold fills my veins. He knows . . . Worse still, he's watching me. I shouldn't be surprised, but I am. I didn't think I meant that much to him. I thought I was just something to pass the time. Clearly, I've underestimated this whole situation.

"Who is he?" he roars in my face, spittle collecting at the corners of his mouth.

I don't reply. What the fuck can I say? I won't put Stoker's life at risk. I won't give him up. Fear claims me, trying to drag me into its ice-cold waters. Instinct tells me this situation is going downhill fast.

"You fuck someone else, little girl?" His fist pulls back and slams into my face. I see stars. "You spread those legs for someone but me?"

He's never been possessive before, never cared what I did as long as I was loyal to the Vipers. This change in direction is giving me whiplash.

He hits me again. My face burns so hotly, the skin tightening over my cheekbones. I'm going to be sick.

"You're mine!"

He lashes out again, and this time, I taste copper in my mouth.

"Say it!" he roars.

I swallow down the blood and I meet his eyes. Defeated. Unable to fight, I do the only thing I can.

The words taste like ash in my mouth, but I'm too scared to say anything else, so I let them spill.

"I'm yours."

5

STOKER

SOMETHING IS GOING on with Layla. To survive prison, I had to learn to read people, and Layla isn't as good at hiding from me as she thinks. Whatever she's into, whatever has her running scared, I'm going to get to the bottom of it.

If she was anyone else, I wouldn't deal with her fucking problems, but it's Layla. Even if she didn't mean something to the club, she means something to me—or she's starting to. I didn't want to feel that connection to her—to anyone—but I can't help it. There's something about her. Something that makes me want things I never dreamed I could have. She makes me think about the possibility of a future, a life. That seemed out of reach before, an idea I could barely touch my fingertips too. I shouldn't be thinking about this shit, not after such a short time.

I text Nox after I leave her flat. He tells me he's at the clubhouse and that he'll wait for me there, so I ride over. As always, being on the back of my bike makes me feel free and easy. I can almost forget the past decade when I'm riding. I let my mind empty of everything but enjoying the open road.

As I pull up outside the clubhouse, I still feel like a visitor, a stranger, even though I'm neither of those things. This world is mine, and I belong in it, no matter what my brain thinks.

I head into the building and find Nox sitting at the bar in the common room talking with Levi. Both brothers look deep in conversation and while I don't want to interrupt shit, this is fucking important.

She's important.

The air feels too thin when I think about shit happening to her, and that hunk of meat in my chest beats a little faster.

I tell myself it's because she's part of the club and Briella's friend, but it's more than that.

I want to take care of Layla.

I need to keep her safe and I'll do whatever it takes to ensure that.

Nox peers up as I approach. The brother is built. He looks like he could crush my windpipe with barely more than a squeeze. All the brothers do, myself included.

"Give us a minute," Nox says to Levi, who instantly pushes to his feet and pats my shoulder.

I didn't know Levi before I went inside, but the guy still treats me like fucking family. That is the way of the club.

Brotherhood.

Loyalty.

Trust.

Honour.

It's why I joined. It's why I remained true to my brothers. It's why I never snitched for a shorter sentence. I would have rather spent two lifetimes in prison than betray my brothers.

These are the rules I abide by.

The code I live by.

If you don't have honour, what do you have?

I take Levi's vacated seat and clasp my hands together on the bar top as I consider how the fuck to broach this shit.

This isn't going to be easy, especially considering my brothers like Layla, see her as part of the club family.

"Talk," Nox demands when I don't speak right away. He's never had infinite patience. That clearly hasn't changed.

"Layla."

"What about her?"

"What do you know about her?"

Nox looks perplexed. "What do you mean?"

"Her past, who she runs with, is she attached?" I have considered the call could have been from another man she's with. Layla strikes me as a free spirit, and I wonder if I'm not the only bloke she's being free with.

I dismiss that idea as soon as it appears. She's many things, but she's not disloyal. I don't think she'd be with me if she was already with someone else. Besides, that call freaked her out. That wouldn't be the case if she was talking to a lover.

Nox's brows draw together as his eyes roam over my face. His jaw slackens. "You've fucked her, haven't you?"

Shit. I don't want to get into what she and I are doing together. It's no one's business, but I don't have a fucking choice. I need Nox's help. I can't do this shit alone. The world has changed too much for me to get the information on her.

I rub the back of my neck, muttering a 'fuck' under my breath. "Yeah, I have," I admit.

Nox rubs a hand over his shaved head, and I can see the frustration in the gesture. "I don't give a shit where you park your dick, but Layla's family. Keep that in mind while you're doing whatever the fuck it is you're doing with her."

"Ain't like that. Ain't using her, Nox. We both ain't looking for more than what we're doing. She knows where shit stands between us."

"I care about the girl. So does Daimon. She's been good to

Brie, to Lucy too over the years. She ain't just some fling you discard when you're done."

Nox's words, his tone makes me more determined than ever to get to the bottom of what's going on with Layla. I should keep my fucking nose out of it. I've got enough crap to deal with, but I saw fear in her eyes when she came out of the bathroom. I saw panic too. Whatever is going on, she's scared to death.

I'm also out of my depth with this shit. I haven't had to look into someone for nearly a decade. I don't even know how it's done these days.

"You think you can do some . . . digging around?" Is it even still called that?

Nox laughs dryly. "Ain't digging around. Layla's good people. Proven herself loyal over the years. Don't need to question her."

"Ain't doubting that, but I just have this fucking feeling in my gut. Trust me, brother. Something ain't right with her."

His whole demeanour changes at my words. "I do trust you. What do you mean ain't right?"

"She took a call while I was there. I saw terror in her eyes, Nox. She's fucking petrified of something, and I want to know what it is."

Nox's jaw tightens. "You think she's in trouble and she ain't saying?"

"I don't know." I shrug. I don't have solid evidence other than that phone call, and that could have been about anything, but my gut tells me differently. It tells me she's into something dangerous. "Could be nothing, but . . ."

"Could be something too?"

"Yeah."

Nox grits his teeth, his eyes flashing at the thought of Layla in trouble. The love she has from my brothers isn't surprising, but it is a relief. I would have fought Nox for help on this, pulled in every favour I could, but I'm glad I don't have to.

"Okay. I'll have a poke around, see what I can find out. You keep this shit quiet, though."

"My lips are sealed."

Relieved that Nox took my concerns seriously, I leave the clubhouse and get on the back of my bike. I've missed riding and use every opportunity to be on the open road. The feel of the air against my face is addictive. It was shit like this I dreamt about while lying on my bunk in prison. There were times I felt like I was never getting out of that hell. I can barely believe I'm free now.

I'm not sure going to Nox was a good idea, but he's one of the few brothers I know on a personal level. I should have gone to Daimon, considering this might impact his girl, but I need to know what is going on first.

I need to know if I need to protect Layla.

It's overkill. I'm being paranoid, I'm sure, but I know how to read people, and she wasn't exactly subtle. Something has her on edge, and I want to know what the fuck it is.

I make my way back to my flat and let myself in. The space feels strange, even though I lived in it for years before I was imprisoned. Everything on the outside feels odd, like an old sweatshirt that doesn't fit as well as it used to. Technology has changed so much. The local area is different from what I remember. Even the club has people I don't know or trust yet to have my back.

I feel like a fish out of water, flopping on dry land and gasping for breath.

The only thing that made any sense is Layla.

Until now.

Now, I don't know where the fuck I stand with her. She's lying, and I fucking hate liars, but I'm hopeful there's a good reason why. A reason I can forgive.

I want to protect her, but I need to protect my club too from whatever has her so scared. If it's something that's going to come back on my family, I need to shore up our defences.

OVER THE NEXT FEW DAYS, the garage keeps me busy. I can't stop thinking about Layla, even though I don't hear from her in that time. Whatever happened seems to have pushed her away from me. It makes me more resolved than ever to discover what's going on with her, so I keep looking into what she's involved with. Nox hasn't come back with anything on Layla yet, but that doesn't ease the tension in my shoulders. That is further compounded by the fact I don't see or hear from Layla in that time. Something is off. I can feel it, so without thinking, I get on my bike and take a ride to her place.

As I pull up outside, that unease starts to grow. I have a good sixth sense, one I trust implicitly, so as I approach the door, ice starts to fill the pit of my stomach. Something isn't right.

I rap my knuckles off the UPVC front and wait.

Nothing.

Where the fuck is she?

I knock again.

Still nothing.

Now, I'm starting to worry. It's completely illogical, but every sense I have is alerting me that something is wrong.

I try the handle, not expecting it to move.

It fucking opens.

Is she kidding me? She hasn't locked her front door? What if I was a maniac? What if I was here to rape her and murder her?

My anger is boiling like a volcano, ready to erupt as I push into the flat. I call her name as I move through her home, searching for her. The living room is empty, as is the kitchen. I pause, not sure I should proceed, but my feet start towards the bedroom. I need to know if she's okay. I need to see her with my own eyes, although the silence of the flat suggests she's not here.

I pause at the bedroom door before I push the handle down and step inside. The curtains are drawn, even though it's the middle of the day, the light struggling to penetrate through them. The room isn't dark, but visibility isn't great either, so it takes me a minute to see the body lying cocooned under the blankets.

Slowly, I step towards the bed and see a swarm of dark hair. It's Layla. Even in the shitty light, I can see her face is fucked up. She's bruised to hell.

Rage like I've never experienced roars through me as one eye opens a slit. The other is so swollen it stays closed.

"Stoker?" Her throat sounds raw as she speaks my name.

"The fuck happened?"

I move to the door and flick the light on. It floods the room and the horror of her face is fully exposed to me. She looks like hell, and my stomach clenches with anger as she sits up, shielding her eyes from the light. Her arms are also a canvas of purples and blacks.

"The fuck happened to you?" My words are hissed out between clenched teeth. I want to put my fist through the wall. I want to rage and destroy things seeing her beautiful skin marred.

She doesn't answer. Instead, she pulls the sheet over her body, but she can't hide the worst injuries to her face. Her cheek is black, swollen and extended, making her pretty face look odd and misshapen. Rage boils through my veins like boiling hot magma. I grit my teeth to stop from exploding.

"Why are you here?" she demands, but her voice is raw, broken even. I've never heard her sound so small. The Layla I've been getting to know is larger than life, ballsy. Takes no shit. This version of Layla fucking scares me.

Whoever laid a finger on her is going to die.

Slowly.

Painfully.

I'm not going to rest until I find out who did it.

"Who did this to you?" I grind out.

"Stoker..." The pleading quality in her voice ticks me off. This shit isn't something she can talk her way out of. I'm not leaving until I have answers.

"Fucking tell me!"

"You need to go." She throws the blankets back to reveal a tiny pair of sleep-shorts and a camisole that does nothing to hide the lack of bra. Neither hides the multitude of bruises covering her skin either. Whoever beat her did a fucking thorough job of it. Red films my eyes as I take in every single mark.

"Who did this?" I repeat, my voice is hoarse as I demand answers. She doesn't move to cover herself, but I can tell she wants to.

"What do you care?"

She's wrong. I care more than I should. She's quickly embedded under my skin, and the thought of someone harming her makes me positively fucking homicidal. "Ain't leaving until you give me an answer. Was it fucking random? Someone you know?"

Her face contorts angrily at my tone. "Why is my life any of your business? Just because we're fucking doesn't mean you get to be involved."

"Because I fucking care!" I roar. "Tell me who touched you!"

Her jaw hardens. "I don't need you to be my white knight,

Stoker. I don't need saving." There's a hint of desperation in her voice as if she's scared to give me more, as if she doesn't want to share the secret of who laid hands on her, but I'm not leaving until I know. Seeing her face messed up like this is playing havoc with my emotions.

I move to the bed and grab her arm. She squeaks at my touch, even though it's not hard, and tries to pull free. I keep a tight hold as I turn it so she can see the bruises. "Every mark on your body will be delivered back ten-fold to whoever did this. You're club. No one touches Sons property."

She manages to drag her arm free and cradles it against her chest as her face contorts into a mask of rage.

"First of all, I'm not 'club'. I'm not part of your world, so I'm not property. And secondly, we're not dating, so you don't get to be involved in my life."

"That ain't your choice any longer," I inform her. "This shit is club business now, and it's fucking mine too." I sink onto the edge of the bed, my fingers trailing over her bruised face. She doesn't pull away, and I take that as a good sign. "Who did this to you? Please tell me."

She winces and glances down. "I can't tell you. I don't want to pull you into my crap."

"I'm already involved in your crap." I was from the moment we shagged. I don't want to admit it, but I'm gone for her.

"You don't owe me that."

"No, I don't, but it's not about owing you, sweetheart. It's about the fact someone fucking hurt you, and that can't stand."

"No one did this to me! It was random. I was jumped, okay?"

She's lying. This was not a random attack. I just don't know why she's holding back, but I'm going to find out.

6

LAYLA

I HATE myself for lying to Stoker. Especially when I can tell he just wants to help but exposing how deep I am with Mitchell is not something I can just blurt out. Mitchell is not a man to test, and if he knows I'm spilling private business, he'll lose his shit. I know Stoker is dangerous too, but he's not a threat to me.

Not directly.

At least, I don't think he is.

He might be when he realises the danger I'm dragging behind me. He'll see me as trouble, see the problems I will bring to the club and he'll walk away. He'll have no choice. That realisation shouldn't hurt, but it does. I don't want more with him, or at least that's what I keep telling myself, but if I'm being honest, I'd admit that isn't the case. I do feel something for Stoker—more than I've ever felt with any other man. That terrifies me even as it thrills me. I've never been particularly bothered about the idea of something long-term. The thought never really entered my head. Men aren't permanent in my world. Never have been. My father taught me that. I don't expect Stoker to stick around when my own dad never did. Trusting people, particularly men, doesn't come easy to me. It's why I'm a love 'em and leave 'em type of girl. Don't get close. I can't get hurt.

With Stoker, I thought for a nanosecond things could have gone further, but I doused it as fast as it reared its head. He's not a man you love. He's the man who rips your heart out of your chest. He's dragging his own share of baggage behind him that I shouldn't want to unpack, but I do. I want to know him every way I can and that is scary.

Because the moment he knows the truth, he's going to do what everyone has done before him.

Leave.

And I'm not sure I can take that. Not from him.

I know he wants answers, but he wants a truth I can't give him. I would give him almost anything else he asked for, but not this. Right now, he's the ringmaster, prepared to face my demons for me, but if he had the truth, this would not be the case. If he knew the truth, he would leave me to hang. They all would, and I wouldn't blame them. My decisions, my choices, brought me here.

I scramble off the mattress, ignoring the pull on my ribs, on my chest. I need to put distance between Stoker and me—a barrier to stop him from getting too close. I need the space, even if it's imagined.

He watches me, his eyes crawling over the bruises I know cover my body. I feel every ache and pain fiercely without seeing the marks marring my skin. For two days, I've been barely able to get out of bed. Every movement is hell. Every twist, tug, reach makes something hurt. I'm still embarrassed at the fact Stoker found me curled up under the covers like that. I'm not a weak girl. I've had to take care of myself for years, but he makes me feel vulnerable, or at least like it's okay to be vulnerable around him.

"I don't believe you were jumped," he says.

Direct as always.

I try to muster some outrage that he doesn't believe me, but since I'm lying, it's not easy. Tired, hurting, and stressed, I throw my hands in the air.

"What do you want from me, Stoker?"

"The truth."

I don't answer. I'm not giving him that, so what can I say?

"Babe, I just want to keep you safe." He speaks so softly, and the endearment makes my stomach fill with butterflies. There are not many men who have been good to me over the years. They take what they want from me, and I'm expected to just accept it. Stoker is no different, despite what he's claiming right now.

I clamp my teeth together and try to hold back the tears pricking my eyes.

"Know you're scared, but we can protect you. I can protect you."

"No, you can't." A tear streams down my cheek, followed by another. The last thing I want to do is cry in front of him, but my grip on my emotions is loosening. I'm beyond overwhelmed. I'm so scared of what I'm facing. I don't know how to get out of the quicksand that's trying to drag me under. How do you defend yourself from a monster?

Because that's what Mitchell is—a monster.

He'd been possessed by darkness when he'd beaten me. There was no compassion in him. There was nothing but rage. He'd seen me with Stoker, and his possessiveness scared the shit out of me. I don't know how long he's been following me, watching my every move, but the fact he is concerns me. I'm not his—at least, I didn't think so. I've never committed to anyone and if I was going to break that streak, I wouldn't do it with Mitchell. The man is a psychopath.

But he thinks we're somehow more connected than I did. He said I was his. It's the last thing I want. The thought of belonging to Mitchell makes me feel fucking sick to my stomach.

He has no compunction about fighting someone who can't fight back. I'm a fraction of his size and I didn't have the strength to stop him. He did what he wanted to, and I was helpless to prevent it. I hate Mitchell for that—for taking away my power, for making me feel weak. For hurting me and leaving me no way to harm him back.

"Sweetheart. Layla. Talk to me."

I peer up at him through watery eyes. How can I tell him the level of stupidity I exhibited? How can I let him fix my mistakes? How can I let him look at me differently?

"I never meant for this to happen."

He doesn't answer, just waits for me to say more. I'm not sure I can. I swallow the bile and start talking. I have to. This might be the only chance I get to let the truth out.

"After Brie moved in with Daimon, I was kind of rudderless. I was alone for the first time in a long time. I didn't handle it well. I kept a smile plastered on my face for the world, but behind closed doors, I slowly fell apart." Shame burns my cheeks and hate claws at my heart. I hate the weakness I showed. I hate it all.

"I don't see how this explains why you're bruised to fuck."

"I'm getting to it," I tell him. I take a steadying breath and continue. "I went a little wild."

His brow cocks. "Wild?"

"I was already pretty heavily into partying, but I took things to a whole other level. I was drinking and doing drugs." I wince as I say the last part. Fuck, I never wanted to admit this shit to anyone. It wasn't the highlight of my life. I screwed up. Without Brie to take care of, I lost direction and sight of things.

His eyes weigh on me heavily as he takes me in.

"What happened?" he asks, his tone softer than I would expect. I thought he'd lose his shit at me.

"I got into debt."

"With who?"

"A guy called Mitchell."

"Who the fuck is Mitchell?"

"Mitchell Webb. He leads—"

"The Crimson Vipers," Stoker interrupts. "Heard of him. Some of his gang were inside with me. Never ran with them. Didn't trust a single fucking one of them. Nasty fucking pricks, though. I understand why Webb wouldn't blink about beating you. You owed them for drugs?"

I nod. "I'm not proud, but I wasn't an addict, Stoker. Not like Brie. I just used recreationally when we partied. It helped me to forget my shitty life, and I was a different person when I was taking them. I felt fucking free. Easy. Different. Taking those pills never seemed like it came at a price. We'd be out at one of Mitchell's bars, and the drinks and drugs flowed like water. I just thought he wanted me to enjoy myself." At Stoker's disbelieving look, I hold up a hand. "I know. I was fucking naive. Stupid even, but I was young and I was living my best life—in the moment. I didn't stop to wonder why he was spoon-feeding me uppers every time I was with him." I pull my bottom lip between my teeth.

"What happened next?" he asks.

I laugh dryly. "He told me I owed him. And it was a lot of money. More than I could earn in a year." I lick my dry lips, trying to get some moisture back, but my mouth is drier than the desert. I can feel Stoker staring at me and his eyes on me makes me feel shame. I should have known better. Nothing comes for free.

"He claim you for that debt?"

"What do you think?"

His face contorts into a mask of anger. "You could have

come to any member of the club. They would have fucking helped. They would have put a stop to this shit before it even started."

I could have, and I thought about it more times than I can count, but ultimately it was my problem. Besides, Brie was dealing with her own shit. I didn't want her involved. I didn't want her worrying about me too.

"I didn't want to let anyone down."

He throws his hands in the air, frustration clear in the gesture. He looks like he's considering exploding like a firework. "Fuck, Layla. So what? You just buried your head in the sand instead? Did whatever that slimy dick wanted you to do?"

"It's not like that!" I protest.

I watch as his mouth pulls into a disgusted, tight line. "You fuck him as part of the debt you owe?"

I wince at the accusation in his voice. "No. Yes." Flustered, I blurt out, "He didn't exactly give me a choice, Stoker. Don't stand there and judge me. I'm terrified of him. You've seen what he's capable of."

The bruises covering my body show he has no issue with harming a woman.

His whole demeanour changes, and I watch the rage burn in his eyes. "He forced you?"

"What do you think? Does my body look like I went there willingly?" I indicate the bruises covering me. "I did what I had to do to survive. You don't get to sit there and look down your nose at me for it."

Stoker roars a curse before he pulls his fist back and slams it into the wall. I flinch as the plaster cracks, but the brick is solid beneath his hand and judging from the misshapen angle of his knuckle and the blood as he shakes his fist out, it did more damage to him. The show of emotion surprises me. I didn't think he cared that much.

"I'm going to gut this Mitchell cunt. I want everything you have on him, and I mean everything, Layla."

Panic assails me. "No. You can't. You'll get hurt."

"The only person getting hurt is him," he hisses. "He touched you against your will. He made you think fucking him was the only way out."

When he puts it like that, it makes shame crawl over my body. "It wasn't that bad. In the beginning, I wanted it. I was happy to have his attention." Mitchell is a good-looking man with oodles of charisma. That changed the deeper I got in with him.

"As soon as that wasn't the case, he should have backed the fuck off."

I wince. "He thinks he owns me."

"He's about to find out how wrong he is," Stoker growls. "I'm going to fix this. No matter what it takes."

It's a promise, and his tone tells me it's one he intends to keep.

"Where are you going?" I demand as he goes towards the door.

He pauses and turns back to face me.

"To fix this, and you're coming with me. Get fucking dressed."

7

STOKER

MITCHELL FUCKING WEBB. She's caught up with Mitchell fucking Webb. She is in deep shit, but I don't tell her that. I ain't scared of the Crimson Vipers. I'll never be scared of anything with my club's backing, but I do know their reputation. It's not a good one, which means I'm scared for *her*.

If that fucker has his claws into her, it's going to be hell to extract her. I need help. I need my brothers. I could do this alone, but fuck, I don't want to. I spent years alone, with no one to watch my back. I need the help.

I keep hold of Layla's hand as I pull her outside and towards my bike. She took her time getting dressed as if she could put off the inevitable, but this shit is happening whether she wants it to or not. We have to fucking protect her, no matter how that looks.

I call Nox, trying not to focus on how she's trembling in my grip. I should have left her here rather than dragging her across the borough, but the thought of her out of my sight makes me want to lose my fucking mind. I need to know she's safe, that Mitchell Webb isn't going to pay her a visit while I'm gone. The thought makes my head want to explode.

He'll never get near her again.

Walking to my bike, I wait for the call to connect, itchy tension crawling along my shoulders as I grip her hand tightly. How the fuck did a girl like Layla end up caught in that viper's nest? She's not an addict—or so she says. I don't think she's lying about that. Addicts can't hide their addiction, not for long. Brie would have recognised the signs in her eventually. No one is that good at hiding themselves.

More importantly, how the fuck doesn't the club know she's tangled in his shit?

Shouldn't they have their fingers on the pulse of this kind of thing? Shouldn't they know who is walking around the fucking clubhouse and the baggage they're bringing with them?

This should never have been allowed to get to this point.

Layla's actions should have been figured out before now. Mitchell fucking Webb should have been put back in his place, and I shouldn't be looking at a broken, battered woman.

I don't blame Layla for the mess she's in. Yeah, she shouldn't have taken the drugs, but fuck, we all do shit we're not proud of when we're young, and she's still young. She's maybe twenty-three or twenty-four—something I should probably know considering I've been inside her. She's younger than me by a good few years as I'm thirty-five, but I don't give a shit about the age difference.

I get her experimenting, trying new shit, and getting caught up in the party scene, but I do blame her for not coming forward as soon as this crap started with Mitchell. She could have stopped this before it became an issue. I know it's hard to ask for help. I'm not a man who does that easily either, but she could have avoided the mess she's created if she'd spoken up.

I shouldn't care.

This ain't my problem.

Layla's just some woman I'm fucking.

Except she's not...

She's more than that. So much more. I want to protect her. I need to protect her. She's mine. No matter what my head tells me, my heart is singing from a different hymn sheet. I feel waves of possessiveness assault me as I think about that cunt touching her against her will.

I want to end Mitchell's life for laying a finger on Layla. Those bruises tell me she was beaten badly. What kind of bastard beats a woman?

Scum bag.

He's going to die for that alone.

You don't lay hands on a woman ever. Don't give a fuck what kind of big shot you think you are. It just isn't the done thing. It pisses me off that he went there in the first place.

"Yeah?" Nox's voice sounds down the line, shattering through my thoughts.

He sounds fucking happy, content. Considering he's got a kid and a good woman on his arm, it's hardly fucking surprising. I hate to ruin his bubble, but this shit is bigger than me.

"Got a problem. Need your help."

"Fuck." Nox lets out a long breath. "Come to the house. Lucy's out and I've got Nora. I can't leave."

Nora is his infant daughter. I've met both her and Lucy a couple of times since I got home. Lucy seems like a good woman. Good for my brother for sure. Perfect old lady material. All the old ladies are.

"I'll be there shortly."

I hang up and walk over to my bike. I turn to give Layla

instruction, but her attention is locked on the chrome. I don't miss the admiration in her eyes as she stares at it. "You like motorcycles?"

She looks like she wants to touch the metal but keeps her hands to herself.

"What's not to like? All that power between your legs. I see why you boys like it too."

She smirks or tries to through the bruises on her face. She's still beautiful, even banged up to hell.

"Ain't why I like riding," I say, snorting a laugh out.

"Why do you?"

"The open road, being on a bike, it's freedom."

"I can understand that," she agrees.

I hand her the helmet that was attached to the lock on the back of the bike. She takes it and glances at it before giving me her gaze again. "What about you? Where's your helmet?"

"Don't worry about me. You need it more. I know how to ride, babe."

Her nose wrinkles, and fuck, I want to be inside her more than ever right now. She's beautiful, with all that luscious dark hair and those dark eyes that see too much—dark eyes that are currently swollen shut and the other at half-mast. She doesn't deserve the bruises covering her body, no matter what she's done. It makes red cloud my vision as I think about how scared she must have been while some cunt smashed his fists against her body. It fucking pisses me off she went through that. It pisses me off that for the past few days, she's suffered on her own, lying in bed because she was too sore to do anything else.

It's not right.

When she told me what she'd suffered, I wanted to lose my head. I wanted to pop my cork like a bottle of wine, but I kept control. I was angry at her for putting herself in that position, at Webb for touching her, at the club for not seeing what was going on.

"What makes you think I don't know how to ride?"

She's been on a bike before? I just hope like fuck it wasn't the back of one of my brothers'.

"Where you a passenger or at the handlebars?"

"Passenger."

For some reason, that makes me want to put my fist through the wall. The thought of her behind another man has me seeing red. Fuck, I don't understand why I'm so fucking possessive over her. I barely know her.

"So, you know how to ride safely?"

"Scared I'm going to get you killed?"

"No. You know how to get on the back?"

All signs of humour flee as her brows draw together. "You want me on the back of your bike?"

The uncertainty that crosses her face makes me frown.

"Unless you want to walk to Nox's place."

Her eyes roll towards the sky as her arms fold over her chest. "I might not be in the life, Stoker, but I know what it means to ride behind a brother. It's not nothing."

I didn't even consider that because, honestly, I want her on the back of my bike. I want her pressed against me, and I don't give a fuck what others think that means. Ain't letting her out of my sight. Not now. That prick turns up, she ain't facing him alone. I wouldn't do that shit to her. I wouldn't leave her to face this demon without backup.

I want to keep her safe. I want to stop this shit from happening again, and if Nox was telling the truth when he said Layla is family, I'll have the full weight of the club behind me when I wipe that dick Mitchell Webb off the face of the earth.

"Get on the bike, Layla."

"Stoker. We can't be more than . . . this."

She waggles her finger between us.

"And what exactly is "this"?"

"Fuck buddies. Friends with benefits. I don't care what label you put on it, but that's all we can be."

I don't want to admit it, but her words fucking gore me. Deep down, on some level, I'd assumed we were making strides. Even though the thought of a relationship fucking terrifies me, I don't believe what we have is meaningless or just sex. When we're together, it feels like so much more. I've fucked a lot of women over the years, even before I lost ten years of my life. It was never the way it was with her. There was a connection. Chemistry. Need. Intensity.

So her words piss me off.

I'm not content to just be her fuck buddy, her friend with benefits. I want to be so much more than that.

"The fuck, Layla? You telling me what's between us means nothing to you?"

I watch as her tongue darts out and wets her lips. "I didn't say that."

"That's what you're implying, though." I scrub a hand through my hair. "Don't try to tell me that sex was just fucking sex. It was more than that. So much more."

"You're getting attached."

"And you're not?" I demand, a little scared to know the answer.

"I can't afford to."

"Why?"

Her smile is a little sloppy, a little sad. "Because you're not going to stick around."

That pisses me off. I hold my arms wide. "I'm fucking here now, ain't I?"

"Yeah, but guys generally don't stick around."

"Ain't going anywhere, Layla. I'm too fucking deep into this now. Know this is new, but if you say you don't feel the chemistry between us, then you're a fucking liar. Ain't never felt anything like what we have. Know we need to explore that further, get to know each other better, but I want you. You don't want to be mine, fine, just say the words and I'll back off, but I don't want this shit to be over yet. Ain't ready for it to end, and I don't think you are either."

Her mouth works as if she's trying to find the words to rebut me, but she can't because she feels it too. I know she does.

I grab her hands and squeeze them gently.

"Babe, I wasn't looking for serious when I got out. I just wanted easy, free. You say you don't want more, fine. I'll walk away right now, but you got to give me those words."

"I don't want . . ."

I hold my breath as I wait for her answer.

"I don't want to stop this thing," she admits. "But I'm scared, Stoker. Trusting you isn't going to be easy."

"Ain't asking you to marry me, sweetheart. Just to give this thing between us, whatever that is, a chance." I step into her space and push her hair off her face. She's still clutching the helmet-like protection between us. "I want you."

"I want you too."

I dip my head and I take her mouth. My whole body shivers as she melts against me. Even despite the mistrust she has, there's a part of her that does want to give into me, and that's heady. I thread my fingers through her hair, needing her closer, wanting to feel her press against me, but the helmet is a barrier between us.

Sucking her tongue into my mouth, I lick around, bracing my unsteady legs. She can't deny the chemistry between us. Kissing her is like touching sunshine. I want more of her. The urge to drag her back into the house and sink into her cunt is unbearable, but I need to sort this Webb shit out. It's only that thought that stops me. I pull back from her. Our mouths are inches from each other, our breaths mingling as we stare into each other's eyes.

"Stoker . . ." She's first to break through the silence, her voice husky.

She's affected by me, and fuck, if I don't like that because I'm slowly becoming consumed by her.

"We need to get to Nox," I say quietly.

I help her put the helmet on and climb on the bike. She gets on behind me in a way that affirms she has ridden before. There's no uncertainty as she scoots behind me. Her hands go to my shoulders, but I pull them around my waist. She feels good behind me, and as her body plasters against my back, I realise I don't want anyone else in that spot —just her.

She clings to me as I start the bike up and pull out of her building parking area. I weave through traffic, taking extra special care as I lane split because of the precious cargo at my back. I never considered putting a woman on the back of my bike, but she feels perfect there. Like she's always been sitting behind me.

Nox lives in a quiet cul-de-sac about half a mile from the clubhouse. It's a nice road, with a small wall and gate at the front of the property. No front lawns, but considering it's London, it's prime real estate.

I stop the bike at the kerb behind Nox's own Harley and cut the engine. Layla climbs off and hands me the helmet back as my feet touch the tarmac.

"Is he going to be pissed?" she asks, nibbling on her bottom lip. The concern on her face makes me want to hit something.

"Babe, no. He's just going to want to help. You don't have anything to fear from Nox."

"I'm not scared of him. I've known Nox a long time, Stoker. I just . . . I feel like I've let a lot of people down."

I lift her chin, and her gaze finds mine. "You ain't let no one down. You just got into a shitty situation that we're going to fix."

"Why?"

"Why what?"

"Are you helping me?"

"Because I want to."

"Stoker..."

I huff out a breath. "Even if we weren't fucking, you're club family. That means something."

"So you're doing this out of a sense of obligation?"

"I'm doing this because I want to. No obligation," I correct her.

"You know this is going to get messy, right? Mitchell isn't going to let me just walk away without any repercussions."

"I know that, but the club'll fix it."

"What if the club can't?" Her voice is small as she says those words. "I'm scared."

"You don't have any reason to be. Ain't nothing going to happen to you, hear me?"

She nods, but I can see the uncertainty and fear still in her face as if she doesn't quite believe my words.

I take her hand. "Let's talk to Nox."

8

LAYLA

I'M NOT scared but facing Nox has my stomach flipping over. The Untamed Sons vice president isn't as terrifying as Ravage or Fury, but I have no doubt he could make me disappear if he chose to. I could easily become a footnote in history. While I trust Stoker on some level to keep me safe, I'm also aware his first loyalty is to his club, not the woman he's fucked a handful of times.

I cast a glance at him as we walk towards what I assume is Nox's front door. In profile, the man is so attractive he makes my ovaries ache. He's all strong lines and his jaw looks hewn from stone. I know what lies under his clothes is just as impressive, and thinking about that makes me want to fuck him again. I need to stop thinking with my pussy and focus on the real issue here.

Without Stoker's help, I'm dead.

Mitchell will not allow me to walk away from this debt he says I owe him. He'll never let me be free. I hate him for that. I hate myself even more for getting into this mess. I knew better. People don't offer you drugs out of the goodness of their hearts. Naively, I thought he wanted to party, and we were fucking at the time, so I thought he was doing me a favour as his girlfriend. I should have known better. Everything comes at a price.

Everything.

It is a lesson I learnt at a young age, one I should have continued to follow. All the men in my life have just taken from me, never giving back.

Stoker doesn't speak as he raps the knuckles of his free hand against the door. I hear movement inside before Nox opens it. He's cradling a fussing Nora in his arms. My fingers itch to take the baby from him, but I'm not crazy—or suicidal.

I'd get away with it with Lucy. Nox... not so much.

Nox's gaze slips from Stoker to me. His eyes crawl over my battered face, anger clouding his eyes.

"What happened?"

"Inside," Stoker says.

Nox's molten eyes find Stoker's again before he steps back, granting us access to the house.

Stoker doesn't release my hand as he goes into the hallway, so I have no choice but to follow. I'd rather be anywhere than here right now. I don't want to see the look on Nox's face when he realises how much of an idiot I've been.

I'm led into Nox and Lucy's small lounge and directed to one of the sofas. The decor is not what I would have expected. Greys and blues, it's a classy look. I would guess Nox had nothing to do with it because this all screams Lucy.

He moves to the armchair and sits in it, shifting the baby in his arms. He's not wearing his kutte, but a white tee that clings to his tattooed biceps like a second skin.

"Someone explain why the fuck you're covered in bruises." No preamble, just straight to the point.

Ice fills my stomach as I feel Stoker squeeze my hand. Nox is going to hit the fucking roof when he finds out.

"I got into a mess," I say.

"What kind of mess?"

"The kind I can't get out of," I explain about the situation with Mitchell in halted sentences. It's difficult to let someone else know how much of a mess I've made of my life. It's impossible to ask for help too. I feel shame run through me as I have to expose all my secrets to a man who has been good to me over the years.

Nox doesn't say a word as I explain. He just listens until I'm finished. Then, he says, "How long's this been going on?"

Too long is the simple answer.

I wrinkle my nose.

"It happened slowly. I didn't even realise what was going on until it was too late. We were just having fun—or so I thought. Then he started attaching all these . . . stipulations."

"You could have come to us." Nox sounds pissed as he says this.

I don't blame his anger.

I could have put the club and any of the old ladies at risk because of my affiliations. I still might have. I have no idea what Mitchell is going to do when he realises his favourite toy has been taken away from him. The Sons are dangerous, but the Crimson Vipers are hardly angels. After I discovered who Mitchell was, I realised just how much trouble I was in. He's got a reputation as dark as any of these men. Darker, in fact, because I know not one single brother would hit a woman. I know because I've watched them with their old ladies over the years. There's real love and respect between them.

"I was scared and embarrassed. Who the fuck wants to admit they allowed themselves to be used like that? I fell into his trap and I was helpless to get out of it."

"Why'd he beat you?"

Fuck. I don't want to answer this. I don't want this to be placed on Stoker's shoulders.

"Layla?" Stoker presses when I don't answer.

"He found out about you. About us." I risk a glance at him and see his jaw has become granite.

"He beat you because of me?"

"I didn't set out to put you in the middle of my messy life. When we connected, I thought it would just be a one-time thing. I thought I could forget about Mitchell and his threats and have something real, something that was my choice for a change. It was stupid, and I paid the price for it."

"Wasn't stupid, babe, and it was real." His voice is quiet, but he might as well have shouted it. My heart flutters at his words, even though it shouldn't. I don't want all these strings attached between us—do I? "Wish you'd told me what was going on, though."

"When was I supposed to do that? Before the first round of fucking—or the second?"

He growls a curse under his breath.

"Mitchell never wanted me," I continue before he can speak. "He wanted the control he had over me. He loved to lord that over me."

He made me do things I can never forget because he said he 'owns me'. Maybe I should have been stronger, maybe I should have told someone and I would never have got into such a mess, but my life was spiralling. I didn't know how to stop it. I was stuck in quicksand and drowning.

Until I met Stoker.

He made me believe I could have normal again—that my life could be more than what my body was worth.

"That cunt is never touching you again," Stoker snarls. "I'll make sure of it."

I meet his gaze. "What are you going to do?"

"End him."

Cold douses me. "You only just got out of prison. You're not going back."

"Babe, he forced you to have sex with him for some fucking made-up debt. Then he beat you for seeing me. You think I'm letting that go? I'm going to make him bleed."

"He forced you to have sex with him?" Nox's quiet voice is lethal. I freeze and swallow down my fear at the crazed look on his face.

"Not at first, but over time, yeah . . ." Admitting that hurts. It makes me feel weak, ashamed. Would any of the other old ladies have done the same? No, they wouldn't have fallen into such a stupid trap. I'd always been reckless, though. Even as a teenager, I was into things that were dangerous. I never had anyone to rein me in. Mum was overworked, doing two jobs to keep the lights on and resented the hell out of me for existing, and Dad was MIA.

I never expected to get burnt by the fire, even though I was close to the flames. In hindsight, it was only a matter of time before it consumed me.

Nox rocks the baby in his arms. "I got to make a phone call."

"You want me to take Nora?" I ask.

He stands and hands me the baby. She's getting bigger with each passing day. Before long, she'll be mobile and Nox and Lucy will have their work cut out for them. I kiss Nora's forehead as I snuggle her close to me.

"I'm sorry I brought this to the club," I say softly.

"Ain't the first one to bring trouble to our doors," Nox says. "Ain't going to be the last. This is what we do. We keep our family safe, and you are family, Layla."

Tears prick my eyes and my throat clogs at his words. I don't expect it to hit me in the gut as much as it does. I never really belonged anywhere until I met Briella. She gave me my first real family. Now, she's given me the club.

I'll always love her for that.

"You should have come to us sooner."

The chastisement makes guilt crawl over my skin. I never intended to hold shit back. That was never my intention. I just felt trapped. Helpless. Hopeless.

"What happens now?"

"I make that call," Nox says.

"To who?"

"Rav to start with."

He leaves the room, leaving me holding the baby. Nora's adorable. She's got wisps of blonde hair and piercing blue eyes that watch me intently as if she knows the turmoil I'm in.

"We'll fix this, Layla." Stoker strokes a finger over the baby's head.

"I know. I just don't want you to end up back inside."

"Ain't going to happen. The club'll protect me."

I want to point out that the club didn't protect him before, but I hold my tongue. I don't want to start an argument."

Nox returns a few moments later, clutching his phone in one hand.

"Rav's called church."

Stoker nods. "Know I ain't an officer. Know I shouldn't be in that meeting, but I want to be."

Nox considers him for a moment. "Okay."

"Lucy's on her way home, so we'll leave as soon as she's back."

"What do you want me to do?" I ask.

"You're coming with me. Ain't letting you out of my fucking sight."

Relief floods me at his words. I'm glad because the thought of being left alone scares me more than it should. I feel safe when I'm with Stoker.

"Okay," I murmur.

Stoker kisses my forehead before turning back to Nox. "I want that fucker dead."

"He'll get what's coming," Nox agrees in a tone that leaves me feeling chilled. There's no warmth there. He and Stoker both look homicidal.

I don't say anything as we wait for Lucy to get back. What can I say? This is going to cause a war and it's my fault. I stare down at the little baby in my arms, wondering if my actions will take her father from her. The thought leaves me cold.

Lucy arrives and comes straight to Nox, her face filled with concern. She's a good woman, a good mother too. I could have talked to her, to any of the old ladies about what was going on.

I didn't.

I only opened up to Stoker because I had no choice and because part of me trusted him. I don't know why he deserves my trust after such a short time, but deep down, I know he's looking out for me.

I know he means it when he says he'll protect me.

We go to the clubhouse. I ride behind him again, trying not to think about what it means to be sitting behind him but loving the feel of his back against me. He feels so strong, so powerful. He could crush me, yet he wants to take care of me.

Nox rides his bike next to Stoker's, the two men keeping close. The roar of the pipes is soothing in a way I didn't expect.

I'm nervous as we approach the clubhouse and cling tighter to Stoker's back. I know I'm safe, that Mitchell's reign of terror over me is over, but I have other things to fear, not just him.

He stops the bike next to Nox's outside the front of the

clubhouse and cuts the engine. I climb off and pull the helmet off my head. He insists I wear it rather than him. As if he won't be hurt if we crash.

He takes my hand and we walk inside, followed by Nox. The common room is busy, and I feel the weight of the stares that find me as we step into the space. I can't hide the beating I took from their gaze, and I don't try to.

Stoker turns and kisses me.

"Wait here. This won't take long."

He disappears into the room where they hold church, leaving me alone. I sink onto the stool at the nearest table. A few of the brothers come to me, demanding to know what happened. I brush them off, not sure if I'm supposed to talk about what occurred yet. I'm glad none of the old ladies are here because I wouldn't be able to hold my silence around them.

After what feels like an eternity, the men emerge from the room. Stoker comes last, talking to Ravage. He nods slowly before his eyes scan the room and lock on me. He says something to Rav and then comes to me.

"Okay?" he asks, his gaze roaming over my face.

I nod. "What are you going to do?" I ask in a small voice.

He smiles, and there's a darkness in that look that chills me.

"We're going to destroy the Crimson Vipers."

9

STOKER

My brothers are angry when they learn the truth of what happened between Layla and the head of the Crimson Vipers. I don't blame their fury. Layla put herself in a stupid and dangerous position, which is infuriating, but she's family and under the protection of the club. That this happened under our noses pisses everyone off—most of all, Daimon. He feels responsible for Layla. She's Brie's best friend, and from what I've heard, she did a lot for her, supporting her through her alcoholism. It hadn't been an easy journey, from what I've heard, and it's something Briella still struggles with to this day.

Fury bangs his fist off the table while Daimon curses under his breath as I finish explaining the situation fully, including the fact that cunt has been forcing Layla to fuck him as part of her debt.

From what the brothers tell me, she's always been wild. She's a girl who likes the party scene and never cared about growing up. She walks along a knife-edge. It was only a matter of time before she got cut. I wish she'd got embedded in something a little less dangerous, though.

I understand why she would be attracted to a man like Mitchell.

Life and soul of every party he's at.

Charismatic.

Dangerous.

Daring.

He'd be a hell of a draw for someone like Layla, who thrives on finding the next thrill.

But that recklessness is the reason she's in this mess—a mess my brothers and me will have to fix because there's no way in hell that fucker is taking anything else from her. I can't judge her choices. We've all made bad decisions in our lives, but I will fix them.

Why?

Because even in the short time I've known her, I've come to realise she means something to me.

She's not a quick fumble, a meaningless shag.

She's more than that. She's under my skin. In my head, and the only word I think when I look at her is 'mine'. That scares me. I've never felt that way about anyone before.

Consumed.

She fills my every waking thought. From the first moment I touched her, I was doomed.

"What the fuck do we do about this?" Daimon demands. I can see how much this shit is affecting him. He's closest to Layla of all the men around this table.

I don't sit on the council, so being in the room where the brothers hold church feels like I've stepped into the inner sanctum—a sacred space I should never have breached. I drum my fingers off the tabletop as my gaze drifts to Ravage.

Prez is a hell of a man, one I'm proud to follow. He's earned my trust, my respect over the years. He always took time to visit me inside. Every month without fail, he'd be sitting in that visiting room. When you're locked up, those moments are the only ones that get you through the dark times. Knowing there are people thinking of you, people who give a fuck, who would fight for you if needed makes a hell of a difference to a person's mental state.

He changed my life.

He gave me the means to keep going when everything felt helpless.

Him and the other brothers who visited. Every week, I'd see a friendly face, would know I was one of them and that kept me going.

On the outside, that respect continues. These men don't have to listen to me, but they do. I asked them for help, and they will give it because I wear the patch, because I pledged myself to a higher cause too. The sanctity of brotherhood still holds firm for me.

"I vote we burn the Crimson Vipers to the ground," Levi mutters. I can see this shit is affecting him. It's affecting all my brothers.

"Why didn't she ever fucking say?" Titch asks, leaning forwards on the table to stare down the length of it at me.

"She's scared of this fucker. He beat the shit out of her just for being seen with me. What do you think he'd do to her if she tried to walk away."

Titch growls under his breath. "Fucking cock."

"He has a hold on her," I add. "He's terrified her into submission. Even now, I don't think she truly believes we can save her from him."

"We'll do that and more," Ravage says. "That fucker and his whole organisation is done."

"Wish she'd spoken to Brie," Daimon says in a quiet voice. "She shouldn't have dealt with this shit alone."

"She's not alone anymore," I assure him.

Daimon's eyes narrow. "Meaning what?"

"She's with me."

He growls. "The fuck, Stoker? She ain't club snatch. You don't get to fuck her and leave her high and dry."

"Ain't what I'm doing." I grit my teeth. Why does everyone think I'm a scumbag who is just going to use and drop her? Yeah, I wanted easy, no strings in the beginning, but I'm not a total cunt. She was also on board with that. Not that it matters, because that ship has well and truly fucking sailed. I want her, and while she was pushing me away in the beginning, she's not now. I can feel her softening towards me, towards the idea of us.

She feels the chemistry between us.

I do too. I don't know how things changed so fast between us, but all I know is that I want her.

And to have her, I first need to protect her from Mitchell.

She'll never be safe while he's still breathing.

"Yeah? So what the fuck are you doing?" Daimon hisses. "She's Brie's best friend. You hurt Layla that's going to upset Brie."

"Ain't going to upset anyone."

Daimon stares at me for the longest moment before his nostrils flare and his eyes narrow.

"I want a go with this fucker."

"As long as I get my pound of flesh too," I grind out.

His mouth turns down, disgust contorting his face. "That she felt she had to give in to that cunt's demands makes me want to tear something apart."

I know how he feels, and I don't know Layla as well as he does. This must be hell for my brother.

The thought of Mitchell touching her heats my blood to terrifying levels I can't control. I want to end his life with my bare hands. I want to rip his throat out and bathe in his blood. I've never considered myself a blood-thirsty fucker, but right now, the desire for revenge is singing through me. I need his end like I need to take my next breath.

"He'll pay for every hurt he put on her," Ravage assures the room. "He touched club property. That ain't standing. Get shit ready for an attack. I want to hit them as soon as possible."

Ravage brings down the gavel, calling the meeting to an end, and relief floods me at his words.

Layla will be safe.

She'll need time to heal from what has been done to her, but she can have all the time she needs as soon as Mitchell is dead.

As I push up from my chair, following the other brothers to leave, Rav signals to me to come to him.

I go to him.

"Until this shit is done, she'll need to stay at the clubhouse. She can use one of the rooms."

The tension in my chest loosens, the elastic band constricting my lungs easing off a little so I can draw a breath. I would have taken her to my place, but the clubhouse has better security, and there are weapons here.

"Thanks."

His mouth turns down a little. "This shit isn't going to be easy to fix. Crimson Vipers aren't some back-alley gang. This could go on for a while," he warns.

He's asking how serious I am about Layla if I'll stand by her no matter what. He's right to ask it, but it pisses me off that he feels the need to. I'm not going to walk away and leave her to deal with this shitshow alone. Ain't nothing that can drag me away from her now.

"I know," I admit. "It needs to happen."

His eyes narrow. "Yeah, it does. Fuck, they think they can touch Sons property without repercussion shit'll just get worse. The fact this has been going on for a while pisses me off. If I'd known..."

He doesn't need to complete the sentence. I know what

he means. This would never have been able to escalate. Not just because we care about Layla, but because no one touches the club without repercussions.

This is about more than her, even if she's the catalyst for what is about to come. If we let one incident slide, where does it end? It's about keeping our family safe. It's about protecting those we love in the only way we know how.

Violence.

Ravage walks me into the common room. "You make it clear to her that in the future, she's to come to one of the brothers if this happens again."

I nod, but the only person she'll be coming to is me.

My gaze roams the room and locks on her sitting alone. She has a drink in front of her that she hasn't touched, and I can see the nerves in the tension of her frame.

As if magnetised to me, her eyes slip around before they find mine. Electricity zings between us. There's this pull I can't explain and don't want to try to. Fuck, I want to be inside her so badly. I want to soothe all her pain with my body. I want to show her how love should feel.

I have no idea why I want to do these things, but it's an impulse I can't ignore. It itches at my skin, clawing at me with each passing moment.

"Call me when we're riding out," I murmur at Rav before crossing the room.

She watches my approach like a gazelle watches a lion. There's wary caution and a hint of fear, but behind it all, I see the need. She wants me as much as I want her. She's just too scared to admit it.

I don't blame her fear. This is new territory for me too. I don't know how to handle what is happening between us. It's moving at light speed.

But in my bones, I know it's right, that what is happening is what is meant to.

Layla gives me a hesitant smile as I approach, and I can see the tightness of her shoulders as I get closer. She's on edge, and while I don't blame her fear, I hope she realises by now that she's safe here, that nothing will touch her while I'm with her. Mitchell is going to die, horribly, for what he's done, and she'll be free to live her life.

"Okay?" I ask.

Her throat works as she swallows hard. I roam her face, taking in every bruise, every cut, every mark.

She nods. "What are you going to do?" Her voice holds a tendril of fear, and that pisses me off. She shouldn't be feeling this way.

I smirk, dark thoughts clouding me.

"We're going to destroy the Crimson Vipers."

Her eyes flare. "How?"

"Don't worry about that part. All you need to know is you'll never have to worry about Mitchell again."

The relief that works across her face makes my blood heat. I wonder how long she's felt the weight of the world on her shoulders. How many sleepless nights this shit with Mitchell has given her? How many times she considered asking for help and changed her mind?

I'm glad this is out in the open now.

I'm grateful to have the chance to fix it before anything serious happens to her. Bad enough, she was beaten, but Mitchell could have done worse to her—much worse.

The thought of her being taken from me makes darkness cloud my vision. I would tear the world apart to avenge her and the strength of that feeling scares me. I shouldn't be thinking this way, not after such a short amount of time together.

I offer her my hand and tug her out of the booth. I don't think. I wrap my arms around her, pulling her against my chest. The feel of her against me soothes some of the rage bubbling in my veins and allows me to breathe unhindered for a moment.

"Ain't letting shit happen to you," I tell her.

Layla shakes her head against my chest. "You can't promise that."

"Yeah, babe, I can. You've got the weight of the club behind you now."

She moves back a little. "They agreed to help me?"

"Yeah." I brush her hair back from her swollen cheek.

"So the club is going to war? Because of me?"

I follow her mouth as she pulls her bottom lip between her teeth. The movement has my cock stirring. Fuck, she's beautiful. Even battered, I can see the beauty in her face.

I need to be inside her now.

I pull her out of the room and down the hallway into a room that's set up as a bedroom—the room we first fucked in. That night seems an eternity ago, another lifetime. It's bizarre to think that what started as a fling, a quick fumble, has turned into so much more. I need her and I think she needs me too.

As soon as I kick the door shut, I'm on her, pushing her against the wall.

She lets out a gasp as I attack her mouth, licking and nipping at her. She smells so good, and my dick is already stirring in my jeans, ready to play with her.

Layla melts in my arms as I continue to devour her. She consumes me like wildfire. I need more of her, no matter how much she might burn me.

I take everything she offers and more, my hand sliding down the waistband of her jeans and into her underwear. She's hot and wet between her legs. I love that she is. I love that I'm making her that way.

I don't think as I guide two fingers inside her while I kiss her senseless.

She moans against my lips as I slide my fingers deeper. She's tight as fuck, and the walls of her pussy clamp around me.

I let my thumb move to her clit to play with that sensitive little bundle of nerves as I continue to slide my fingers in and out of her. Her whimpers are pushing me over the edge. She sounds like heaven, and the slight part of her lips as she sucks air in is doing things to me.

I need to have my cock in her, but I want to make this good for her. I'm patient, bringing her to climax before I shove her jeans down. She's still gasping for air as I get her to step out of them. Her underwear follows until she's just standing in her tee.

I drop to my knees and put my mouth to her clit. Her fingers sink into my hair as she twitches her hips. I flatten my tongue against her, and she groans as I lick around her sensitive bud.

"Stoker..."

I don't stop licking, and I can tell within minutes she's close to going over the edge again. I widen her legs to give me better access and cling to her thighs as I continue to work her up to fever-pitch. She's panting heavily, her little mewls of pleasure making my dick so hard it's almost painful.

She goes over the edge with a cry of ecstasy, her thighs trying to squeeze my face between them.

I get back to my feet and lift her. Carefully, I place her on the bed like an angel, her hair fanned around her face. She drags her tee off and frees her tits from the confines of her bra, then lies back on her elbows. There are more bruises covering her body, marks that make me want to lose my mind. Even with those injuries, she's fucking beautiful. Her dark nipples and pert breasts that are enough for a handful tease me.

I move over her and duck my head to take a nipple in my teeth.

"Stoker!" she gasps my name, and I can't help from smirking.

"What do you need, babe?"

"You."

"Me?"

"I need you to fuck me."

Her dirty words elate me. I want to fuck her too, so I palm her breast before pushing up and shoving my jeans down my legs. My boxer briefs follow, my cock freed from my clothes. I run my fingers over the shaft before giving it a couple of tugs. Tingles spread through my balls, through the base of my spine as I grab a condom from the bedside drawer, grateful someone keeps this room stocked, and open the packet. She watches me with heavy, sultry eyes as I roll it down my cock, her thighs widening in anticipation of what I'm about to do to her.

I don't hesitate. As soon as the condom is in place, I go to the edge of the bed and drag her down it, so she's in the perfect position. Then I rub myself through her wet folds and push inside her.

We both groan as I enter her pussy, sliding into the root. Her eyes lock to mine, and I see the desire in them, the consuming passion. She wants this and more. I understand it. I feel the same.

I start to move my hips, building a rhythm that makes my balls start to feel tighter.

"Harder," she whispers.

"Don't want to hurt you, babe. You're still banged up."

"Fuck me harder, Stoker," she orders.

I do as I'm told. I slam into her with a renewed force. Our sweaty bodies connect as I hold her hips to keep her in place. Fuck, I'm going to come fast. This isn't going to be a long session. My desperation to have her makes my cock feel like steel.

I hold her tight, my grip bruising as I continue to fuck her as she asked.

Hard.

I see the need in her eyes. The same is probably reflected in mine.

Her pants become more desperate as she climaxes, and I follow her a moment later, spunking into the condom.

For a moment, my vision winks out as I groan. When it comes back online, I peer down at her. Cheeks flushed, hair tumbled, she looks gorgeous. I bend down and kiss her mouth.

I'm never letting anything bad touch her again. I don't care who I have to kill to keep her safe.

10

LAYLA

I lie wrapped up in Stoker's arms, my pussy sore and deliciously used by him. I feel safe. For the first time in a long time, I feel like nothing can touch me. Nothing can hurt me.

I'm with Stoker because I want to be. Not because someone is holding it over my head, not because I have no other choice. I picked him. It's a liberating feeling. I love the feel of his body wrapped around mine, his strong arms cocooning me.

"Stoker?"

"Yeah, babe?"

"I don't want you to get hurt."

"Ain't going to."

"But Mitchell has it out for you. You've taken his favourite toy away."

"That prick won't get near me, Layla. The club'll watch my back."

"Mitchell is crazy."

"You think I'm not crazy too?"

He strokes his fingers up my side, a relaxing gesture that is at odds with his words.

"I think you're a kitten." It's a joke. I know he's a dangerous man. I can see the effects of his prison term on him. There's a darkness that swirls in his eyes, and the way he carries himself tells me he's used to having to watch his back. There's a wariness in his swagger.

I understand it. Prison can't have been easy, especially considering his club affiliations. Those links would have kept him safe, even as they put a target on his back. Who wouldn't want to take a swing at a member of the Untamed Sons just to look like a big shot?

"Babe . . ." He grins at me.

"I'm scared." The admission is harder to give than it should be. I'm not someone who is used to being vulnerable, and right now, I feel like I've sliced my chest open so he can see my thrumming heart.

"I know, but ain't letting shit touch you. Everything will be okay, Layla, I promise."

His assurance calms me a little, and I snuggle deeper against his side.

"What happens now?" I ask.

"Rav and the others will come up with a plan and we'll execute it."

"And Mitchell?"

"Don't ask that question if you don't want to hear the answer."

I swallow down my words. I know they're going to kill him. What other choice is there? They leave him alive he's going to come after me—possibly the club. They're sticking their nose into Mitchell's business, and he's not going to like that. He's going to be pissed enough I told someone what's happening.

Fear clutches my heart in a clawed hand, squeezing so tightly my chest aches.

Stoker must sense my apprehension. He strokes my hair off my face.

"You've got nothing to worry about. This'll all be over soon. I promise."

"You still want me after this?" My voice is thick with emotion, my words clogging my throat as I force them out. Tears sting my eyes and I will them not to fall. I can't allow it. I've already shown too much weakness, too much vulnerability.

"Babe." His tone tells me I'm being crazy. Maybe I am, but I need the assurance right now.

"Well?" I demand.

"Yeah, Layla, I still want you. That's never been in doubt."

"Even though I'm damaged goods?" I hate how small I sound, how pitiful. I don't want to be this person. I'm strong. I'm resilient. I'm not some cowering damsel who needs to be saved, except that's exactly what is happening. Stoker is riding in on his white horse to save the day.

"Fuck," he mutters under his breath. "You ain't damaged goods. I hate that prick for making you believe that."

I trace patterns on his bare chest. There're a few tattoos covering the skin, and I wonder about the story behind them. Maybe one day he'll tell me.

"I am sorry," I tell him. "I never meant to bring my troubles to the club's door."

"You still don't get it, do you? You are club, Layla. The brothers accepted you as one of us. What happens to you affects us too. You're club property. The moment Mitchell touched you, he signed his own death warrant."

I want to rebut his statement that I'm property, but I don't think this is the right time to go on a rant about feminism and not being owned like a prized cow.

Besides, it means a lot to me that these men see me as family because that's how I see them. Coming to club cookouts is my favourite part of the month. I love spending time with the old ladies, with the kids. No matter how many times I've seen it, Titch's snatch and tits apron still makes me laugh. This is home, and it's been that way for a while now. It's the place I feel most comfortable like I can be myself without any judgement.

Stoker is a complication. What if things between us turn sour? I don't want to lose what I have with the club.

"We shouldn't do this." I sit up, tucking my hair behind my ear. My ribs pull as I move, but that's not why there are tears in my eyes.

"The fuck are you talking about?"

"This is going to get messy."

"Babe, it's already fucking messy."

"I don't want to lose the club," I blurt.

"Why in the fuck would you lose the club?"

"If things go bad between us, I'll be the one out in the cold, not you. This is all I have, Stoker. This is my world as much as it's yours."

He scrubs a hand over his face, and as I start to move off the bed, he snags my wrist. "Firstly, this shit ain't going sour. Get that idea out of your head right now. I don't know where this is going, but I know that when I'm with you, I feel different. You quieten the voices in my head. Make it easier for me to breathe. When I first came out of jail, I felt lost. I don't feel that when I'm with you."

His words make me choke up. Fuck, I can't believe he's saying this, that he even thinks this way.

I should be terrified, but I'm not. I'm strangely at peace with him, like this is meant to be this way. He puts all my demons to bed, makes me forget the fear that always stalks me when I think about settling down with someone. He makes me feel safe.

Neither of us speaks as we lie entwined in each other's

arms, two halves of a broken whole. I don't want to think about the danger he's going to face. It scares me to death. Mitchell isn't some small-time playground bully. He's terrifying. It was that fear that bought my silence about what he was doing to me. I was too scared to cross him. Now Stoker and the other men are going to war—because of me. This is what I hoped to avoid. I never wanted to drag anyone into my problems. I don't want anyone else forced to pull my baggage behind them.

My phone starts to ring from my jeans pocket. I ignore it, not wanting to move out of Stoker's embrace. It cuts off then starts jangling again.

Fuck.

I don't want to move, but I only know one person who would call me, hang up, and call again.

Mitchell.

"I better . . ." I break off as I untangle myself from Stoker and climb out of bed. Naked, I go to the crumpled pile of my clothes and rummage until I find my phone. The name on the screen confirms my worst fears. It's Mitchell.

I feel Stoker move at my back. "It's him," I murmur, my heart pounding like a steel drum.

"Answer it. Don't let on that anything is different."

Easier said than done when everything has changed. I know the brothers are coming for Mitchell. I know these will be his last days breathing. How am I supposed to talk to him knowing that?

I swallow the bile and swipe my finger over the screen to accept the call. Stoker presses the speakerphone button.

I barely get a "hello" out before Mitchell is barking down the line at me.

"Where the fuck are you? I need my cock sucking."

Stoker's lip curls into a snarl, but he keeps silent.

"I've been busy. I have a life and a job."

It's the wrong thing to say. "Your only job is pleasing me, you stupid bitch. Need you here."

My gaze flicks to Stoker, who is clenching his jaw so tightly he's going to break his teeth if he's not careful. He shakes his head.

"I can't," I say into the phone.

"Wasn't asking. Get your fucking arse here. If I have to come and find you, I'll do more than beat you."

The line goes dead. Pain lances through my chest before Stoker pulls me against him.

"He dies tonight. I'll kill him myself."

11

STOKER

THE CALL from that bastard leaves my blood boiling. The way he speaks to Layla makes me want to cut his fucking dick off and feed it to him. He thinks he owns her.

He's about to discover how wrong that assumption is.

I call Ravage as soon as Layla hangs up on Mitchell and explain what's going on. This is going to speed up our timeline. We can't risk him trying to find her. She's safe in the clubhouse, but we need the element of surprise. That means we need to act now.

Ravage tells me he's coming back to the clubhouse and that he's going to call the others in too. That eases some of the fear crawling through my veins. Knowing my brothers will be here soon allows me to relax a little. They will do everything to protect Layla.

Her phone starts to ring again and she jolts like she's been struck by an electric current. I move behind her and glance at the screen. Briella.

"I don't want to answer it," she admits.

"Why?"

"Because she knows the truth, and I'm not ready to face her."

I slide my fingers around her nape and pull her close to me. Kissing her, I let everything I feel for her leach out of me, telling her without words how much I want her.

"She's your friend. She's not going to judge you."

Layla bites her bottom lip before she slides a finger over the screen to answer the call. I watch her as she moves away from me to talk. I let her have her privacy and head into the bathroom to shower.

It'll take about half an hour for everyone to get back to the clubhouse, so I take my time washing. When I go back into the bedroom with a towel slung around my hips, Layla is sitting on the bed in her tee and thong. She makes me stop in my tracks. My eyes roam over her body, and fuck, I want to take her again right now.

There isn't time.

I have to fix this shit with Mitchell fucking Webb and then we can build our lives. She's mine, and I'll take as much time as it takes proving that to her. I won't let her push me away, even though I know she's scared of taking a risk with me. I can tell she's got hurt in her past, which has closed her off. I need to open her up again. I need to make her see that I can be trusted. I might be a bastard, but I'm a bastard who is completely consumed by her.

"Brie knows," she says. Her voice cracks as she speaks, and I can tell it's taken a lot out of her talking to her.

"Babe, your friends just want to help you."

"That's what she said." A tear escapes from her eye and rolls down her cheek. Anger fills me that she's sitting here crying because of that prick. I'm going to enjoy torturing Webb. I'm going to make that fucker beg and I'm not going to give him any mercy. I'm going to make sure he suffers. For every bruise he's put on Layla's skin, I'm going to revisit tenfold on him. I'm going to make him squeal like a little pig because that's exactly what he is—a pig.

I wipe Layla's tear and lean down to kiss her. "After today, you won't have to worry about that prick anymore."

She snags my wrist. "I worry about you."

"I'm going to do whatever it takes to protect you. I don't care what that entails, babe. Mitchell Webb has breathed his last."

I don't miss the relief that clouds her face.

"Thank you."

I kiss her, my lips brushing over hers gently, my fingers caging her face. I want to get lost in her, but I have to go. I need to meet up with my brothers.

"Stay here," I tell her. "Don't leave the clubhouse for anything."

"Okay," she agrees.

"I won't be long."

Her smile is wobbly. I press my mouth to hers again. I let her sink into the kiss before I force myself away. Parting is difficult. I want to stay in this room and fuck her all day, but I have to leave.

Before I can change my mind, I snag my kutte off the hook on the back of the door and shrug into it. With a look back at her, I leave the room.

I make my way to the common room, my mind blank of everything except the rage pounding through my veins. I keep focused on the task, trying not to let my emotions overtake my sense. I need to keep a level head. I need to be ready for the upcoming fight.

Levi is the only brother waiting already. He eyes me as I enter the room, peering up from his seat at the bar. He gestures me over.

I push around the tables to come to stand at my brother's side.

"How's Layla?"

"Holding up," I tell him.

"This shit'll be over soon."

It will, and Mitchell Webb and his Crimson Vipers will be a thing of the past.

The other brothers start to arrive shortly after. Ravage is among the last to get here, with Fury not far behind him. We file into the room we use for church, all patched members, not just officers, and as soon as the doors are closed, we start to discuss what we're going to do.

I listen to the plan, and then we make our way out to the van. The element of surprise means we're not going on our bikes. Instead, we're taking two white vans filled with brothers. I spot Pleck as I climb into the back of one of the vans. The man has been good to me, helping me settle back into the garage, teaching me the ropes like some rookie kid.

I take a seat on the floor of the van between Titch and Daimon while Rav gets in the passenger seat and Levi takes the wheel.

Titch hands me a gun, and every instinct in me recoils from taking it. This was the shit that got me locked up in the first place. It represents ten years of my life gone. The last thing I want is to touch a fucking firearm again, but I need protection against what is going to come. I need to keep myself safe and watch the backs of my brothers.

"Know you don't want to take it, brother, but you're going to need to be armed going up against the Vipers," Titch says as if reading my thoughts.

Hesitantly, I reach out and wrap my fingers around the handle, taking it from Titch. The world doesn't implode. Nothing terrible happens, but my heart squeezes so hard I feel like I'm going to have a heart attack. No way in fuck can I go back to prison, not after finding Layla, but I have to make things safe for her, and that means getting my hands dirty.

The drive to the Crimson Vipers' headquarters feels like it takes forever, and as the building comes into view, adrenaline starts to heat my blood. I want my pound of flesh and my body readies for the upcoming fight.

As soon as the van stops, everyone piles out. I don't see who enters first, but we swarm the building like locusts. Fuck, these idiots are dumber than a box of rocks. No security, no one to stand between them and an attacker. They deserve everything they get.

The sound of guns discharging fills the air, and the coppery-iron smell of blood is thick in my nose. In the chaos, I try to keep a bead on the kuttes of my brothers, careful not to hit any of them in the crossfire.

I shoot a man near to me, the bullet slamming into his neck, spraying blood in an arc. I don't give a second thought to the fact I just took a life. I don't care. This is for Layla, and for her, I'd kill a thousand men.

As I twist, I see a man lining his weapon in Nox's direction. I don't think. I let off two rounds. He goes down heavily, the side of his skull exploding in a mass of blood and tissue that splatters up the wall to the side of him. I don't watch him fall, my attention moving to the next victim.

I put bullets in more men as they surge forwards to attack us, and I can barely breathe through the smell of death. As the dust starts to settle, I peer around the room, making sure my brothers are still standing. There's a couple of injuries, but nothing major, which makes my pulse slow its staccato beat in my chest.

I lower my gun but don't put it away as a man is dragged forwards between Daimon and Titch. He struggles against their hold, fighting to get free, but both men hold him steady, their grips unrelenting. Even if the fucker gets away, he's completely outnumbered.

My nostrils flare like a raging bull as I take in his flickering gaze. He's nervous, and he has good reason to be. Most of his men are dead or lying in pools of their own blood, writhing. We're about to wipe his entire organisation off the face of the earth.

And him with it.

Mitchell fucking Webb.

I have no doubt it's him. Even beneath the anxiety, there's a 'fuck you' attitude. As the leader of the Crimson Vipers, he's a man used to being obeyed.

He's about to be demoted.

My blood starts to heat as his eyes find mine, and then his mouth pulls into a snarl. He recognises me. He knows I'm the fucker Layla's been seeing.

His eyes flash fire.

Fuck, I want to put a bullet in his head right now, but that would be too fast, and this cunt needs to suffer.

My gaze travels to the rings on his fingers and the chains around his neck as Daimon and Titch dump him on the floor in front of Rav. Mitchell's dark hair is shaved close to his scalp, leaving a dark stubble covering his head. I can't see any tats, but he's wearing a heavy leather jacket that hides most of his rangy frame from sight.

Fury stands next to Ravage, and I notice he twitches his finger on the trigger of his gun, ready to throw down if necessary.

Nothing will touch Ravage.

All of us would take a bullet to protect him.

"The fuck is this about, Ravage?" It's bluster. His eyes dart around the dead, and the colour drains from his face.

Rav grinds his jaw, and I see the monster come out of the box for a moment. "Layla Hargreaves."

Mitchell's brow wrinkles, and I can see he's genuinely confused.

"What about that snatch?"

I don't think. I react. I cross the space between us and my fist snaps out and slams into his jaw, sending the prick sprawling. The satisfaction I feel from seeing that isn't something I can put into words.

"She's fucking Sons property and you touched her," I roar. More than that, she's fucking mine, and for touching her, I'm going to flay the skin off his fucking bones. "You're dead."

I drag his head up with an iron grip on his chin and spit in his face. He barely flinches, but his mouth turns down into a snarl.

"Look into my eyes, fucker," I growl. "They're the last thing you're going to see before I carve your dick off."

He lets out a sharp laugh. "You think that bitch is worth going to war over?"

I shake my head. "Look around, Mitchell. We already fucking won the war. Your men are dead and we're taking everything you fucking own. You're dying today. There's no doubt about that. I'm going to enjoy every moment of hurting you."

I see the flash of fear as he's dragged to his feet by Titch and Daimon. I'm going to enjoy my moment with him in the club's kill room. I know Fury isn't going to like being pushed aside. He's our resident torturer, I've learnt since I got home, but this is my fight, and it's one I'm going to see through.

I want his head on a platter.

Mitchell's hands are bound at the base of his spine before he's shoved into the back of the van. The rest of us pile in, leaving the chaos behind—a blood bath and a message not to come at us to others who might consider it. I take my seat again and lock eyes with Mitchell as my mind mulls over all the shit I'm going to do to him.

"You should never have laid a finger on her," I hiss at him.

He doesn't speak, just glares defiantly at me as the van starts to move.

By the time we reach the clubhouse, my skin feels like a thousand fire ants are crawling over me. I need the release I know is coming. When I bleed this fucker, some of the tension I'm feeling will leach from my pores.

As the van pulls to a stop, I meet that fucker's gaze and let all my darkness swirl into my eyes. I'm going to enjoy every minute of torturing this cunt.

I follow as he's dragged through to the kill room. It's a dark, dank space that is designed to elicit fear. There's a bare bulb hanging from one side of the room that casts more shadows than it does light. It does in Mitchell. His eyes roll around the space, his jaw tight as Titch and Daimon string him up on the hook attached to the ceiling.

I move to the side of the room and shrug out of my kutte. Ravage steps up beside me as I hang the leather on one of the coat hooks on the wall.

"You sure about this? Fury can do it if you ain't feeling up to it."

"Fuck no. I want to do this," I assure him. No one is delivering this shit but me. Nothing else will soothe this beast inside me.

He nods and glances over his shoulder at Mitchell. "Make it hurt."

I go to the cabinet that holds all the implements Fury uses to torture and open the top drawer. There are various knives, pliers, and a few other contraptions I'm not sure how to use.

Fury leans against the wall, Nox and Daimon joining him. It's just the four of us and Mitchell, whose breath is tearing out of him in ragged pants. Fear is starting to set in. The realisation that this shit is happening and there's no way out for him.

He's dying in this room.

My face will be the last thing he ever sees. I pick up what looks like a blowtorch, turning it in my hands.

"You want some advice?" Fury asks.

Since the man is a master torturer, I say, "Yeah."

"Direct it at the feet. It'll hurt like fuck."

I grin. "Perfect."

It doesn't take me long to get the blowtorch lit. The glow of the flame bounces off the walls as I move towards Mitchell.

Without preamble or warning, I guide it to his foot and the smell of burning flesh is punctuated by his visceral screams.

12

LAYLA

I BITE my nails to the quick, waiting for Stoker to get back. Alternating between moving to the window and sitting on the bed, I would imagine I'm giving myself a good workout. Nervousness tingles through me. Did they find Mitchell? Did Stoker get him without getting hurt? Did everything go according to plan?

I know his brothers will have his back, but it still doesn't stop me from worrying. This situation isn't exactly normal, and I have no clue what to expect.

Eventually, I'm forced to lie on the bed. My body is stiff, sore from my beating and pacing is not helping. I curl into a ball on top of the covers and let myself drift off. I don't know what else to do but wait. Stoker told me not to leave the clubhouse, and while I could head down to the common room, I don't want to fend off questions about my bruises.

The door opens, and my gaze slides towards it as Stoker slips inside the room. His hair is damp, his clothes different than the ones he left in, but there is a lightness to his step that wasn't there before.

I start to sit up, unsure what I'll find in his eyes. Will there be demons staring back at me or will they be clear?

I meet his gaze and see nothing. They're blank. Unreadable. That scares me more than seeing the darkness in them.

"What happened?" I demand.

Stoker comes to the edge of the bed and sits on it. The mattress depresses under his weight before his fingers sift through my hair.

"Are you okay?" he asks, ignoring my question.

"Stoker, what happened?" I'm determined not to be derailed by him. I need to know if Mitchell is gone. I need to know if I can sleep easily or if I need to look over my shoulder.

"Mitchell Webb is no longer a problem."

He kisses me. No, it's not a kiss. It's more than that. It's like he's consuming me with the power of his tongue alone. My body feels weak to resist him. I don't want to either. Whatever he's offering, I want it. I want it all. I've never been open to a relationship before, but with Stoker, it doesn't seem scary.

His fingers clamp around the back of my neck. "You're mine," he tells me, his words hard, unrelenting. He's not going to take no for an answer. Good thing I don't want to disagree with him.

"I'm yours," I agree.

He pulls at my clothes, undressing me like I'm a doll. I let him take from me, wanting him inside me, needing him to fuck me. I should care that he's fresh from murdering a man, but that thought doesn't penetrate through the fog of need.

I part my thighs as he comes between my legs, his hardness pressing against my pussy. The barrier of his jeans against my bareness is annoying, and I can't help from rubbing against him like a cat.

"Fuck me, Stoker."

He lifts off me and disappointment floods my veins until I realise he's only moving so he can get out of his jeans. Good. I want his cock. I need to feel him. This isn't going to be sweet—not that it ever is with him—but it's going to be fast and dirty.

He drags his tee over his head and uses it to tie my hands together.

"What are you . . ." I break off, my gaze finding his as confusion wars for dominance.

"Do you trust me?"

"Always."

He pushes my bound hands over my head. "Don't move."

It's an impossible request because the moment his cock probes at my entrance, my hands itch to touch him. I keep them locked in place, even though I want to move desperately as he slides deep inside me. My pussy stretches around him, and there's a bite of pain, a pinch as he pushes further.

Fuck, I feel so full, so overwhelmed by the sensations surrounding me as he starts to piston his hips. I lie still while I adjust to him. As soon as I'm healed, I want to ride him, but right now, I don't think my body could take it, so I settle for letting him do all the work.

My breath rips out in shallow pants as my eyes lock to his. The electricity that crackles between us is overwhelming. I want him more than I've ever wanted anything in my life, and as scared as I am of committing to him, I'm more scared of letting him walk away.

"Okay?" he asks.

I nod. "I won't break."

His hand roams over my belly, the bruises stark against my pale skin. "I don't want to hurt you."

"You won't."

He fucks me hard, his movements verging on pain. My

orgasm crashes through me like a wave of pleasure. I gasp out his name as he spills inside me with his own grunt.

My body feels boneless as he pulls out of me and rolls off me, careful not to put any weight on me. I whimper at the loss of him.

Both of us lie still, breathing through the moment. The back of my neck under my hair feels clammy and there's sweat beading on my skin. I need to shower.

"Didn't use a condom," he mutters, breaking through the moment.

He didn't. It takes me a second to realise my thighs are sticky and that I'm leaking his cum from my pussy.

"Shit," I say, draping an arm over my eyes. "I'll get the morning-after pill."

Neither of us is ready for more right now. We need to get to know each other better first before we risk bringing a child into our relationship.

He nips at my lip. "You're fucking beautiful."

He's being kind. I look like a patchwork of bruises and cuts. Even though he did all the work, I feel exhausted and my chest aches.

Despite how I feel, I peer into his eyes as he looms over me, careful not to give me his weight. "You're not so bad yourself either, handsome."

His tongue sweeps over my mouth, begging entry, and I give it to him. He devours my mouth like a starved man, taking everything I offer and more. The kiss he gives me leaves me fighting for air. It's like he sucks all the oxygen out of the room. If I were standing, my legs would tremble and I'd have to sit down. Fuck, he makes my whole body sit up and take notice. It's like the heat is infusing my body, burning my skin.

When he pulls back, we're both breathless. He leans up on his hands to peer down at me.

"Did I hurt you?"

I shake my head, my heart full. Men never care about me. They just care about what they can get from me. I'm usually nothing more than a convenient hole to fill, and that was how I think Stoker went into this thing between us. I was someone to pass the time with, someone to get off with. I went into it with the same mindset. I wasn't looking for Mr. Right. I wasn't looking for anything but a fun time.

I don't know when feelings changed, when the no-strings-attached idea was discarded, but Stoker wants me. I can see it in his eyes. There's affection there, shining back at me. He's hard and stubborn, difficult at times and possessive, but he truly cares about me. That's not something I've experienced with a man.

"I'm fine," I assure him. I don't want him to have guilt about what we did. I don't have any. I feel completely and utterly sated.

His fingers trail over my throat before sliding lower to run over my breasts. I whimper as his thumb rubs over my nipple.

"I can't keep fucking you like this while you're healing from your beating," he says.

I suck in a breath as he lowers his head and sucks the bud into his mouth. My fingers find his hair, pulling him closer.

"I'm fine if you do all the work and I just get to lie here."

I am sore. Every inch of me hurts, but we both needed to get lost in each other for a little while. Things have been difficult the past few days since I spilt my secret about Mitchell. I didn't think I'd ever survive what he was doing to me. I was sure I'd end up dead. With Mitchell, there was never any other outcome. How I got there depended on him and what mercy he might have shown, but Mitchell isn't known for his mercy—wasn't known...

I push it out of my head. Mitchell isn't my problem

anymore. I don't care if he's dead. I know I should. He was still a human being, but he made his choices and what he did to me was cruel. I know I was stupid, taking drugs from a man like him, but I thought on some level he cared about me, that he wanted me to have a good time. I should have known it came at a price.

He kisses me, making my body shiver.

"Mine," he murmurs as he palms my body.

"Yours," I agree.

13

STOKER

Layla spends the month healing. The dreams come almost instantly after Mitchell's murder, nightmares that snap at her heels, leaving her jack-knifing out of bed. It guts me to see her in this state. When she's catapulted awake, she clings to me like I'm life-saving driftwood, and I pull her close, holding her against my chest until her breathing evens out again.

She needs to talk to someone, but she's reluctant to do it. I get it. She was coerced into sex by a total bastard who used her in the worst kind of ways. Who wants to admit that? But her mental wellbeing is more important than her embarrassment.

It isn't me who gets her to see a shrink, but Briella. Daimon's old lady puts her in touch with the therapist she used after she was raped. It relieves some of the pressure in my chest, knowing Layla is going to talk to someone. She needs to let this shit out and work through the feelings of shame she has.

While we wait for the appointment to come around, I stay at her flat every night, holding her when she wakes up screaming. It fucking kills me to see her like this. I wish I could take her pain for her.

It's probably not the best idea to start up a relationship with her. She needs to heal, but there's no way in hell I can walk away. I mean it when I say she's mine. She is. The thought of being without her makes my stomach fill with lead. I won't give her up, not now that I've had her.

My gaze goes to the mirror over her dressing table as I lean against the door jamb. Her makeup is smoky, sultry, heavy, and her lips are a bright blood red that makes my cock hard as I imagine how they'd look wrapped around my shaft. She's wearing a tiny leather mini skirt with her shit-kicker boots that reveal her legs. A few weeks ago, they had been covered in bruises too, but most of the damage has healed now.

Every day, I think I killed that cunt too fast. I'd tortured him for hours. I'd let Fury have his turn, too, knowing that fucker could do shit I wouldn't even think of. By the end, Mitchell was blood and urine-soaked, a shell of a man. I'd carved at his skin, burnt him and done worse. I took great pleasure in every stroke I made, every wound I inflicted. He deserved so much worse than I gave him. I should have kept him alive for days, taking him to the brink of death only to bring him back again, but I'd wanted to get back to Layla, and that desire made me move faster than I should have.

Mitchell did beg for mercy in the end.

They all do, but I never gave it.

He didn't deserve any.

He hadn't given Layla an inch of mercy when he'd used her as his own personal fuck toy when he'd beaten her.

I push the encroaching darkness out of my thoughts as her gaze slides up towards me. I want to kiss her all over.

"No," she says.

"No?"

"I can see what you're thinking from the look in your eyes and we don't have time to fuck right now. We're already late."

"Whose fault is that?" I ask, amusement lacing my words as I watch her fluff her hair. I don't even care that it's taken her over an hour and a half to get ready. All I care about is her happiness, and right now, she looks content. That makes the bands in my own chest loosen.

"It takes time to look this good," she says around a smile.

She's not lying. She looks stunning. The little halter top she's wearing draws my attention to her tits and I can't stop looking at them.

"Eyes, Stoker." She cocks her head at me. "We've been sleeping together for over a month, and I don't know your real name."

I laugh. "Stoker is my real name. My surname anyway. Name's Graham Stoker."

She repeats the name, rolling her tongue over the syllables.

"It suits you."

I move behind her, pulling her hair over her shoulder so I have access to her neck. Dipping my head, I pepper kisses along the column of her throat. She tips her head to the side to give me better access.

"Babe, we don't have time for this," she protests weakly.

"Make time."

She whimpers as I suck and nip at the skin, my hand slipping under the material of her halter top to find a bare breast. No bra. Easy access. Yeah, I can get behind this.

I massage her tit as I continue to suck on her neck.

"Don't leave hickeys," she says around a moan.

That sound goes straight to my balls and fuck, her words make me want to leave marks on her more than ever.

She opens her legs as my hand drifts south, sneaking under that tiny little skirt that has risen up her thighs. I push her underwear aside and move my fingers through her folds. She's wet already, ready for me, and fuck, if that's not making me want to bend her over and pound into her right now. I always want to fuck her.

I didn't think there was anyone who could quieten the voices in my head, the ones that kept me locked in prison still. I never thought I'd assimilate back into society, that I'd find a sense of worth again. Things changed too much. I changed too much. Prison did a fucking number on me.

Then I met Layla and she turned my world on its head.

With her, I feel alive again. It's almost as if I can breathe uninhibited. She makes everything feel easy. I've never felt so right in my own skin. Not until I met her.

Layla has fast become my reason for breathing. Spending time with her eases the tension from my bones, makes me forget the past decade and the hell I suffered. I didn't think life could be good again. I was wrong.

I slip a finger through her folds and push inside her slick heat even as I continue to kiss her neck.

"Stoker..." she gasps my name, and it's an instant jolt to my cock. My name on her lips will never get old.

I bring her to climax, my fingers pistoning in and out of her slick cunt as she pants. She trembles before turning to me and giving me her eyes, and fuck, I want to get lost in her.

"I want your cock in my mouth."

Her words make me harder than titanium. My dirty girl. She turns on the chair, her fingers moving to the belt of my jeans. She rubs me through the material, and I suck in a breath. If she keeps this up, I'm going to blow in my boxers.

She frees my cock, peering up at me as she does. I cup the side of her face before fisting my fingers in her hair.

The first swipe of her tongue over the head of my cock makes my hips twitch. She takes me fully into her mouth, and my balls tighten. Shit, this isn't going to last long.

She licks, sucks, and nibbles at my cock until I'm panting hard. I brace my hand, not in her hair, against the back of the chair and close my eyes as she sucks my dick like a fucking pro.

The slurps and sounds she's making are driving me crazy. I want to be inside her. I want to fuck her pussy hard and fast, but we don't have time for what I want to do with her. The party started an hour ago. We're already fucking late.

This will have to suffice.

My hips buck, breaking through my thoughts and my balls draw up. Then I spunk down her throat. She swallows me down like a good girl, wiping at her mouth as she does. She's a wet dream.

She smiles at me, and something eases in my chest.

"Fuck, I love you," I breathe the words out in a rush.

Her smile fades as her eyes flare. "You . . . you love me?"

I shouldn't have blurted them like that, but the intensity in my chest tells me my words ring true. I do love her. She's the jagged half of my broken edges. We fit together, even if we're both shattered and damaged. I need her in my life, and that wave of possessiveness I always get with her attacks me.

Mine.

She's mine and she'll always be mine. I knew that before I gave her the words, and from the look on her face, I should have given her them before now.

"Yeah, babe, that isn't obvious?"

"Not to me. I've never been loved before—not unless you count Brie. I know she loves me."

I silence her with a finger to her mouth. "Ain't sure where you came from, sweetheart, but ain't ever giving you up. I'd walk into the fires of hell for you."

She leans forwards to kiss me then stops. "I should probably brush my teeth first." Her lopsided smile makes me grin.

Fuck, I kiss her, not caring that I can taste myself on her lips.

"We're going to be even later," I warn as I pull her off the chair and walk her back to the bed. I go down on top of her, and for the next thirty minutes, I make love to my woman.

EPILOGUE

LAYLA

SIX MONTHS LATER...

I stare at the positive pregnancy test as if I can make the second line disappear.

I'm pregnant.

How the fuck am I pregnant?

We use condoms every time we fuck, and that has been a lot over the past six months, but pregnant? Seriously?

I duck my head between my knees and try to breathe. I'm too young to have a baby. I'm not ready. My mum was shit; how the fuck am I going to be a decent parent? I don't have any yardstick to measure success by.

"Babe? We need to leave." Stoker's voice outside the bathroom door makes me jolt. Fuck. I stuff the test into the box and shove it in the bin, hiding it under empty toilet rolls as if that can hide the evidence. It can't.

Things with Stoker have been nothing short of a dream. I've been in therapy, dealing with my trauma, and he's been with me every step of the way, helping me and loving me for me. He's been amazing with me, and honestly, I'm so in love with the man it's unreal. I can't breathe without him, but having a baby is such a huge step. Is either one of us ready for it?

I guess we have to be.

I nibble on my bottom lip as I try to consider how to tell him we're having a baby.

"Layla, Brie, and Day are here," he yells through the door. "We need to get going."

Fuck, fuck, fuck. Between them, both my best friend and my boyfriend they're going to figure out something is wrong. They're like bloodhounds.

I can't hide this. I'm not even sure I want to. I try to make sense of the emotions rolling through me, and the one shining through most clearly is panic. It's followed by a tendril of hope. I'm happy, right? I want this. The timing isn't perfect, but yes, I want this. I want my baby.

I place a hand to my stomach, wonderment washing through me.

I'm pregnant.

I'm having a baby.

With Stoker.

A man I love more than life itself.

Yeah, I'm happy.

I open the door, and he's waiting on the landing, leaning against the wall. He peers up as I fill the doorway.

"Okay?" he asks, and I can see the worry on his face as he scans me, checking for anything that might be of concern.

I nod. "Yeah. I'm uh . . . I'm pregnant."

It's not what I mean to say, but they are the words that spill from my mouth. Keeping secrets isn't me. Not anymore. I saw the damage secrets did when I was hiding Mitchell from my friends. My therapist would be so proud of me right now for opening up like this.

His eyes flare. "You're pregnant?"

"I just did a test and—"

He doesn't let me finish. He crosses the space and presses his mouth to mine. As always, my heart starts to race under his touch and I melt against him, unable to stop myself. I love him. We're having a baby. This is good news, and from his reaction, he agrees.

Breathless, Stoker pulls back and presses our foreheads together. "We're having a baby." It's not a question but a statement, and I hear the happiness in his voice. Stoker's life was put on hold while he was locked up. Although I know he's taken things slow with me, so I don't meltdown, I can tell he's pleased by my news.

"Is that okay?" I ask.

"It's better than okay, babe." He closes his eyes. "Marry me."

His words leave me feeling like I'm standing on shifting ground. "What?"

"Marry me."

"I'm already yours." And I am. He'd put his property patch on my back as soon as he could. "You don't have to put a ring on my finger as well."

"I want you to have my last name, Layla. I want my kid to have my last name. I want us to be a real fucking family."

I kiss him. "We are a real family."

"So marry me."

"Okay."

He brushes his lips against mine. "We could skip the party," he says, a wicked glint in his eyes and I know that look. He wants to take me to bed and fuck me.

"When we get home, you can do what you like to me, but we have to be at that party."

It's an anniversary party for Sasha and Ravage, and it's important. Though my pussy does pulse at the thought of Stoker dragging me back to bed.

I kiss him. "Brie's waiting."

We head to the party, neither of us able to stop grinning, shooting each other glances when we think no one is looking. Neither of us wants to take the sparkle off Rav and Sash's day, so we keep our news locked down. Six months later, we welcome our daughter to the world.

Elicia Rose Stoker.

GET A FREE BOOK AND EXCLUSIVE CONTENT

Dear Reader,

Thank you so much for taking the time to read my book. One of my favourite parts of writing is connecting with you. From time to time, I send newsletters with the inside scoop on new releases, special offers and other bits of news relating to my books.

When you sign up, you'll get a free book.

Find out more here:

www.jessicaamesauthor.com/newsletter

Jessica x

ALSO BY JESSICA AMES

Have you read them all?

UNTAMED SONS MC SERIES

Infatuation

Ravage

Nox

Daimon

Until Amy (Until Series and Sons Crossover)

Levi

Titch

Fury

Bailey

Stoker

Cage

FRASER CRIME SYNDICATE

Fractured Vows

The Ties that Bind

A Forbidden Love

UNTAMED SONS MC MANCHESTER SERIES

Howler

Blackjack

Terror

IN THE ROYAL BASTARDS SERIES

Into the Flames

Out of the Fire

Into the Dark

IN THE LOST SAXONS SERIES

Snared Rider

Safe Rider

Secret Rider

Claimed Rider (A Lost Saxons Short Story)

Renewed Rider

Forbidden Rider

Christmas Rider (A Lost Saxons Short Story)

Flawed Rider

Fallen Rider

STANDALONE BOOKS

Match Me Perfect

Stranded Hearts

ABOUT THE AUTHOR

Jessica Ames lives in a small market town in the Midlands, England. She lives with her dog and when she's not writing, she's playing with crochet hooks.

For more updates join her readers group on Facebook:
www.facebook.com/groups/JessicaAmesClubhouse

Subscribe to her newsletter:
www.jessicaamesauthor.com

- facebook.com/JessicaAmesAuthor
- twitter.com/JessicaAmesAuth
- instagram.com/jessicaamesauthor
- goodreads.com/JessicaAmesAuthor
- bookbub.com/profile/jessica-ames

Made in the USA
Coppell, TX
08 April 2022